COLORFUL LIES

Editor: Michael Part
Proof editor: Michele Caterina
Copy editor: Yaron Ginsberg
Cover design: Mirko Pohle
Inside page layout: Lazar Kackarovski

Library of Congress Cataloging-in-Publication data available.

This is a work of fiction. Names, characters, places and incidents either are the product of the author's imagination or are used fictitiously, and any resemblance to actual persons, living or dead, businesses, companies, events or locals are entirely incidental.

Published by Sole Books, Beverly Hills, California.

Printed in the United States of America

First print edition May 2020

www.solebooks.com

COLORFUL LIES

by
Daffodil

To Otto

I LIVE A LIE

My name is Alexa "Daffodil" Goldsmith and I am eleven years old. I live in Beverly Hills, in a mansion at the top of the hills. You may have seen it on TV.

My father writes for the movies. But most of the time he just stares at the page.

My mother is an interior designer, but the last time she designed a house it ended with a lawsuit because her clients couldn't find their bedroom.

What she really does for a living is star in a reality show.

But you may already know that.

I have one half-brother.

At least this is what they tell me.

Our family is a mess. We are on a slippery slope and I'm the only one who can save us from total destruction.

What would you do if you found out that you live a lie?

What would you do if you found out that your parents had lied to you your whole life?

Your mom, the most wonderful, loving mom in the world.

Your dad. The strongest, smartest, nicest dad ever.

I was six when I heard my mom yelling at him: "You're a liar!" and I thought I understood what I was hearing. It was the first time, of many to come.

Then she threw a glass of red wine in his face.

He sniffed the wine that was dripping all over his face and mumbled, "Chateau Laffite '86 was a great vintage." But Mom wasn't amused. She demanded a confession.

At first he denied all of it. He swore that he was telling the truth, the whole truth, and nothing but the truth.

But at the end he said in a trembling, pleading voice, "I'm sorry, darling. I'm sorry that I lied to you."

My mom lies too. All the time. And I'm not including the fairy tales she told me when I was little. The fluff parents feed their kids about angels, fairies, and witches. Those are stories adults make up to make their kids feel better and go to sleep happy and fast. And maybe it makes adults feel good for a while, before they have to go back and deal with the real stuff in their own lives, the stuff that makes life so much harder. And no fairy is around to answer their wishes.

While they tell their kids sugarcoated stories, they don't seem to care that one day their kids will come to their senses and realize that these were just a bunch of lies packaged with a sweet voice and a smile. When you are little you are not supposed to deal with life's real stuff. You get some time before it lands in your face. Unfortunately, there are kids in the world that don't have this grace period. They get it hard and nasty right from the start.

So this is why our parents are forgiven for lying to us, and when you have your own children you'll tell them the same stuff. You have to.

This is how it works. But if you wish to look at the world as it is, no sugarcoating and filters attached, you don't have to go far, because the world is in the palm of your hand, whether you like it or not.

Check your smartphone.

My mom has perfected the art of lying. When the liar and the lie become one, when the liar becomes immersed in his or her lie, he or she believes that their lies are the truth.

My mom is Luella Walker Goldsmith. You might know her as Luella, or by her nickname—Cruella.

She had just sent me a text asking why I wasn't ready. She is nervous, and so am I. Cruella's crew is waiting downstairs for me, with their cameras ready to roll.

I hope I survive.

I look at myself in the mirror: Nothing to write home about.

Why write home when I'm at home anyway?

I wear jeans and my favorite purple t-shirt with the words, "Leave me alone or die!"

I put on the Catwoman mask. It looks neat, in my opinion. I glance at my notes on my smartphone. I know exactly what I'm about to say.

Let's go Daffodil.

It's show time.

A WHITE LIE

Dad: I love your mom, she is the best mom in the world.

Me: And what about Michelle, your private trainer?

Dad: What about her? She is no longer my trainer.

Me: I saw you kissing her and touching her, and heard you telling her that you love her.

Dad: Well, sometimes we say things we don't really mean. And we hug people... it's normal. Are you sure you saw us?

Me: Yes. A bunch of times. Just last week in the swimming pool, and later in the kitchen.

Dad: It's not what it seems.

Me: What does that mean? Is it true or not?

Dad: Yes. I can't lie to you. But sometimes you need to tell white lies. *White lies are as important as the truth, because you tell them in order to not harm the people you love.* Like your mom.

Me: I see. Daddy, can I tell you a white lie?

Dad: Sure, go ahead, sweetie!

Me: You are the most awesome Daddy in the world!

He looked baffled and didn't know if it was okay to laugh, so I immediately said, "Just kidding, I love you, Daddy!" and I saw the tension fade away from his face.

Men. They never grow up.

My dad is sweet. But people say behind his back that he is weak and spineless. His dad, Grandpa Hilton, says that Dad is a weasel. It's not very flattering, and I'm not happy to hear it, but I'm afraid there is some truth to it. I think he is a nice person who caves in to pressure too easily and doesn't stand for his principles. He lets other people rule him. And, as can be seen on TV, when you are surrounded by strong, controlling, and cruel people, you can't be weak. They'll destroy you. But Dad found a way to deal with it. And as long as the supply of his favorite medicine isn't cut short, he's fine.

My dad's name is Harold. He hates his name, but no one ever found him a suitable nickname. So I guess he got used to it.

A BEIGE LIE

My mom always told me that the most important thing in life is to be happy.

"Why?" I asked.

"Because being happy is the ultimate goal of all human beings," she said, with the know-it-all tone she had mastered.

"Why?" I asked.

She thought about it for some time, but was too lazy to get into the subject. "It just is. When you grow up, you'll get it."

When she can't explain something, she always tells me to grow up.

And guess what? I am growing up. And my brain is growing up fast, and it tells me that my mom is not exactly the deepest thinker on earth.

My mom would not have been able to come up with, "I think, therefore I am."

She would have gotten stuck at "I."

Maybe that is too much to ask of her. She is better off with "I am, therefore I think... sometimes."

Anyway, I never let go when I want to show people how shallow they are.

"And what do I have to do in order to be happy?" I asked her.

"You need a lot of money, for starters," she said firmly, and immediately corrected herself. There was a mist in her eyes that threatened to wipe off her mascara.

"No. You actually don't need a lot of money to be happy. I was the happiest person on earth when I was young and poor. But when you get older, it gets important."

"To be happy or rich?"

She looked at me confused for a moment, and then she said in her assured manner, "Happiness can't make you rich, right? But money can make you happy."

She looked a bit surprised at herself, having come up with such words of wisdom. "I need to write that down! I'll use it in the show!" she said victoriously. "Darling, bring me a pen and paper, will you?"

"Happiness is important," my dad agreed. "Why?" I asked.

"Because when you are happy, you feel good," he said. "Don't you want to feel good?"

"Are you happy?" I asked. "Yes, I'm happy," he said.

"Why?"

"Because I'm successful, I have a wonderful family, I'm healthy, and so on." He looked bored. I knew he was saying it just to get me off his back. But I wasn't on his back. I was sitting on the carpet in his backyard office.

"But just the other day I heard you telling Mom that you are unhappy," I reminded him.

I knew I had embarrassed him, because his face turned red and he began looking for the bottle of Jack Daniels that was hidden behind his cabinet of screenplays.

"Sometimes I'm unhappy. It's normal," he said in a low voice. "Everyone is."

"Why?"

"Because there are things in life that make you unhappy. Most of the time you just want to be happy. But it's tough to *really* be happy."

"Why?" This question has been my trademark since I started to talk.

"Because there are so many things that are not that good in life. And some are really bad. That's why. Besides, no one really knows what happiness is. It is hard to define."

"Mom knows," I said. I liked to pit them against each other. It was fun.

I saw the twitch on his face. The twitch that always appeared whenever I mentioned her.

"Mom knows? Is that so?" he couldn't hold back the sarcasm, and I knew he regretted it the second the words left his mouth. He was desperate for a drink, but he promised Mom not to drink in front of me. His knuckles turned white as he tried to keep his hands from shaking.

"So Mom lied to me?" I demanded, without giving him an opening from which to withdraw.

"She didn't lie to you, she just sugarcoated it a bit." "It's a white lie?"

"It's an off-white lie," my dad smiled and eased up a bit.

"What do you mean?"

"Well, for example, when people meet each other, they often say, 'It's so good to see you.' But most of the time they don't mean it. But it doesn't hurt anyone. It floats and bursts like a bubble in the air, and that's it."

"A *beige* lie," I said.

"Exactly," my dad laughed and hugged me.

I mentioned already that he was the nicest man on earth. That is why so many people like him, but no one seems to appreciate him. Because in this world being nice isn't something people consider important. Being nice is something people admire if it comes with being smart, successful, rich, and handsome.

This is Beverly Hills, after all.

THIS IS REAL

Mom gained her celebrity status in the reality show, *The Rich and Beautiful Women of Beverly Hills,* better known as *RBW90210.*

Our beloved city, which is known all over the world as the home of the world's top celebrities, began as a Spanish ranch where lima beans were grown. Now, 34,290 inhabitants roam around with fancy cars, and have no idea just how boring the place looked when the city was born in 1914.

And if you are looking for lima beans on Rodeo Drive— forget it!

My mom is still pretty, although she is forty-five years old. Or, in her count, somewhere in her late thirties. Some years ago, she decided that one year stretches for twenty-four months. I'm not supposed to talk publicly about her age, but I personally think there's nothing wrong with being forty-five. Unless you feel it's wrong.

She once said that her pregnancy ruined her waistline, and from there it had been an uphill battle.

"You shouldn't have brought me into the world," I said. "I ruined your body."

She smiled and said, "Oh, don't be silly," which made me think she didn't totally disagree with me.

Anyway, it was too late for both of us.

In the show, she loved to praise Dr. Gold, whose magic scalpel kept her looking gorgeous. She also liked to say that she had never much cared about her looks. "I humbly accept it," she said. Of course no one believed her. I thought it was laughable and embarrassing, but people didn't correct her. Because her lies were part of the fun people had when they watched the show.

Everyone knew she was a liar, and they inhaled every word she uttered because people are willing to be lied to when it makes them feel good.

Like so many women in our town, she spends a huge amount of time and money trying to look great. She says that it's part of her job, otherwise why bother? But I knew that every wrinkle on her face and every additional ounce of weight made her angry and worried. If you ask yourself why Dr. Gold is on the show so frequently, you would not be wrong in assuming that my mom receives free treatment in return for promoting him.

There is another lie. It's our family's biggest secret.

We're broke.

We were rich. But not anymore. We are, as my dad put it, "On a slippery slope minutes before plunging into the abyss."

I heard him telling that to Mom and my brother, Ian. One afternoon, he even told me.

The door to the office, a shack in the backyard where he locks himself in and tries to write the next Hollywood blockbuster, was half open, which was unusual. I knocked, and when he didn't respond I pushed it open and entered.

"Hi Daddy," I said. I wanted to get out fast, because the stench was horrible. There was an empty whisky bottle on the desk, and I knew he had been drinking.

"Come over here, sweetie," he said in a tired voice. "I want to give you a hug."

He hugged me so tight, I couldn't breathe.

"How's your writing going?" I asked as soon as he let go.

"My writing stinks, thanks for asking." He looked miserable. "I'm doomed. I'm done. I can't write anymore. I don't think I ever could, but whatever talent I may have had, it vanished for good."

"You are not supposed to talk like that, ever!" I told him. "People might believe you!"

"I know, sweetie, I'm terribly sorry," he mumbled. "I'm not feeling very well."

"Mom said that when you hit the bottle, you can't write," I said, hoping that he would straighten up. It was too much for me to handle. But I knew I couldn't leave. Not now.

"She's right," he said gloomily. "I need the bottle to get going, but my writing gets worse when I drink. It's a vicious circle."

"So maybe you shouldn't write. Try reading, it's much easier," I quipped.

I come up with these half-stupid jokes because they always make him laugh.

He laughed, but his laughter turned suddenly into a sob. "I'm sorry, sweetie, I feel like crap." A tear rolled down his cheek.

He looked really bad, and I got worried.

"I can't give up writing," he said, and wiped his tears with a tissue.

"Why?" I asked. I wanted to hug him, but I also wanted the conversation to continue. If I hugged him, he would feel even more sorry for himself.

"Because writing is everything to me," he said. I knew what was coming because I had heard it many times before. "In addition to you and your brother, whom I love the most," he quickly added.

"And Mom!" I reminded him.

"And Mom." He looked as if he wasn't sure.

Why was writing so important to him? Obviously it made him miserable. I didn't quite get it, although it was clear to me at my tender age that people craved things that made them unhappy. They wished for the things that killed them, but before it killed them, it made their lives miserable.

By the way, these aren't my words. I'm just quoting someone much older and smarter than me.

I knew that my dad was going downhill because I heard Libby, my parents' personal assistant, saying stuff about Dad to her fiancée over her car phone when she was driving me to school.

"Since his last huge hit, that forgettable vampire movie he wrote five years ago, everything he comes up with becomes box office poison," Libby said.

Box office poison!

Everyone knows that poison is something you die from. So it was clear to me that if dad's writing made people die, he certainly shouldn't do it for a living.

I asked him about it, and he turned all red and yelled at me, "Who told you that?"

"I read it on the internet," I said.

That is how you get away with this kind of stuff. You blame the internet.

I was lying to protect Libby. A white lie. Remember?

"You aren't supposed to read all that nonsense!" he cried out.

"But it was you who gave me my first iPhone when I was four years old," I reminded him. "What do you expect?"

He threw his hands up in despair and cried, "Everything is so out of control here!"

'Out of control.' This phrase is at the top of my 'no-fly zone' list.

It represents everything that is wrong with our world. If things are going your way, then everything is in control. But if your life has crashed into pieces as a result of your own poor choices, then it's *out of control*.

More words on my 'no-fly zone' list: *'LOL,' 'literally,'* the words *'and then'* and *'like'* used more than twice in one sentence. And *'honestly.'* I hate that word, honestly.

Mom and Dad like to fight in the kitchen, where they can have a bite and a glass of wine before they get crazy and begin throwing stuff at each other, smashing the fine china to pieces.

This is their quality time together.

They don't care much about the mess they leave behind, because Gabby and Rosie, our two maids, clean the scene after they're done and gone.

When Mom informed Dad that she'd gotten a phone call from her agent offering her a job on a reality show, it was clear to me that it would end in a big fight. I made myself comfortable in my favorite spot, overlooking the kitchen, hidden behind a naked statue of Aphrodite, one of the many fake art items scattered around our house. If you question the authenticity of the beautiful, armless Aphrodite, you'll be told with a straight face that it's a replica of the original. Fake isn't a welcome word in our household.

The conversation between my parents over turkey sandwiches and white wine deteriorated quickly into a shouting match.

"Agent? Since when do you have an agent?" my father fumed.

"Since a week ago," Mom said, arching her brows. "You have an agent, why shouldn't I?"

"I'm a writer, for Christ's sake!"

"And I'm a socialite," she said calmly.

"Since when is being a socialite an occupation?!" he yelled.

"Since forever," Mom enjoyed torturing him. "It started in ancient Egypt."

"Really?"

"Yeah! I Wikied the subject thoroughly," she said. "Anyhow, I got an offer to star in *The Rich and Beautiful Women of Beverly Hills.*"

He looked stunned.

"A reality show? Are you nuts?" he cried out.

"Why are you so against it?" Mom looked excited, her green eyes glowed with pride.

"I hate those shows," he said, trying to stay calm. "It's about shallow, useless people aimed at even shallower, more useless people. The worst thing that happened to television ever! It's degrading, an insult to one's intelligence. You can't possibly do it. It will ruin whatever is left of our reputation."

"They gave me a very intelligent offer," Mom said calmly. "And we need the money, *as you probably know.* Just last night you said that we won't make it through Thanksgiving."

He looked at her for a long moment, letting the words sink in. "How much?" he asked faintly, his red eyes all lit up.

"The base salary is fifty thousand per episode," Mom said victoriously. "They got a twelve-episode order, so it's not too bad, is it?"

Dad looked pale and confused.

Mom would later say that he was jealous.

At least she got an offer. He hadn't gotten any offers for the last two years.

It was too painful to watch. Even behind the fake statue of Aphrodite.

"They can do better," he said finally. "It won't be enough."

I heard him once saying that we need at least a quarter of a million a month just to stay afloat.

"Oh, they will," Mom smiled. "I will make this show a hit, and those stingy bastards will open up their wallets and come up with the dough."

My dad looked torn. Mom waited. She gave him time to arrive at the right conclusion. She knew him well. As much as he hated her job offer, she could see the dollar signs blinking in his eyes.

"My only concern," he said in a more intimate tone, "Is that I'm not sure it's going to make you happy." He always came up with the right words to make him look good.

He was a writer after all.

"I want to do it because it will save us from a financial disaster," my mom said in an icy tone, "Not because I like it." She wasn't letting him change the subject. He was supposed to bring money to the table. Loads of money. But he failed to do so, and she wanted him to know that, from now on, she would be running the show. She would rescue the family, and it had nothing to do with her happiness. Because she wasn't happy, and it was all his fault.

She had to be rich in order to be happy. And when she married him, he was a successful screenwriter and the son of a billionaire.

How can one go wrong? Apparently one can. One can go *very* wrong.

My dad didn't like what Mom said. I saw it in his eyes when he left to go to his backyard office in the shed. He reacted the way he does in every argument. He just didn't say anything. He let it go.

It was safer for him. But I knew that, inside, he was hurting.

Mom's new career move gave our family a much-needed lifeline.

Remember what my dad said? That we are steps away from plunging into the financial abyss? He knew perfectly well that Mom's new show could save us. But Mom had a grander vision. It wasn't only about the money she would be getting from the show. It was about becoming a national household name.

Because in America, being famous can get you a lot of money.

You don't have to be smart.

You don't have to be nice.

You don't have to do something for the common good of your fellow man.

You don't have to do anything worthwhile.

Just sit back, relax, and let the camera roll and make yourself famous.

When America loves you, the money begins to flow.

But Mom didn't do it only for the money. It was so much more than that. She really wanted to be famous. She wanted America and the rest of the world to love her.

While she roamed through the house—which the show called a mansion—the viewers could never figure out what was behind the glitzy setting. She looked beautiful and rich. And all across America, people were sitting in crummy living rooms watching her, moving elegantly through our fourteen bedrooms and six bathrooms, which were spread over ten thousand feet. She was living the glamorous life that was everyone's dream. And no one could tell that she was on the verge of a financial breakdown.

A RED LIE

The source of our soon-to-be-gone fortune was Grandpa Hilton. He was now living in an old folks' home on Burton Way where I visited him once a week. He was always happy to see me. We met in the lobby and took the short ride to Joan's On Third, our favorite hangout.

Grandpa Hilton told me that he was going to die soon, but this did not mean that I had to eat so fast.

"I'll wait until after you finish the muffin and the chocolate milk. I promise you!" he said, winking.

At first his humor was scary, but I got used to it and eventually I really liked his wit and wisdom.

"If you die here you'll kill their business for an hour or so," I told him, pointing to the bustling joint.

He laughed, and I knew what was coming. "You are the smartest Goldsmith around, other than myself, that is," he said.

The three of us sat together outside, on the sidewalk, enjoying the cool breeze. Grandpa, his Filipino nurse, Joe, and me. Our driver, who in Mom's show is called 'the chauffeur,' though his real name is Carlos, was waiting for me in the car.

Grandpa thought that people in general were pretty stupid. Once he said to me, "Even the smartest people are stupid. That's how God designed us."

I remember it vividly. We were about to leave his nursing home, and he raised his hand and pointed to the residents who were scattered in the lobby. "Look. Most of them used to be bright and now they don't know who they are anymore."

"But you're still sharp," I told him.

"Not for long." He sighed.

Dad was the youngest of Grandpa's three sons. "I failed as a father," Grandpa confided to me. "All my kids are losers."

"Even Daddy?" I asked.

"Your dad is the nicest of them all," Grandpa said. "But he is a loser nonetheless."

Grandpa never told me that he loved me, but I sensed that he did. And I knew he meant it when he told me I was special.

I came up with another colorful lie, one that's most commonly used when people utter the word love. No word is so much used, abused, and overrated. If you happen to listen to the lyrics of a song that do not include the word 'love,' something is probably wrong.

When people use the word 'love' in vain it should be named a red lie.

Maybe something is wrong with me. You might call me a cynic. I have never felt love, and I often wonder if most people really even know what it means. I have a warm feeling towards people: Dad, Grandpa, my brother, and even Mom, when she is not annoying. But if this is love, I wonder what all the fuss is about?

I hope that when I find out what love is, I won't be bothered with long speeches about it.

You want to kiss? Just kiss. Don't waste my time telling me how much you love me. But I suppose I'm too young and too inexperienced, so maybe I've got it all wrong.

And no one has ever kissed me before. I think that should be changed when I'm ready, of course. And I think I might be ready when I'm twelve. It seems the right age for a girl like me, because everyone tells me how mature I am.

But if the would-be kisser starts sounding like a lousy pop song, I'll definitely tell him to shut up.

Although—and this is totally confidential—there's a guy that I'm curious about. His name is Justin, but I nicknamed him 'The Knight.' He is handsome, tall, and smart. And two years older than me, which is perfect if you ask me. He plays basketball and soccer, and he has long dark hair and dark eyes. I love his smile, and he's so darn funny. He's in a private school somewhere in LA, not part of our wonderful Beverly Hills school system. Not in my school, which is right opposite the Beverly Hilton Hotel.

I never met him, and I'm not sure I ever will. We're just friends on Facebook and Instagram. I'm not sure he even knew who I was when he accepted my friend request. I saw a status he posted on a mutual friend's wall and liked it, and that's how I got to know him. I think I know quite a bit about him, but he doesn't know anything about me. This is how 'friendship' goes these days. You become friends with a total stranger whom you've never met and might never meet. It's weird. But then again, the entire world is weird. Maybe it used to be better. Before smartphones and social media and the internet. But that was so long ago, in a different century, and I can only imagine how people interacted with each other.

Face to face! Are you kidding me?! That's so bizarre!

Back in the day, humans couldn't avoid talking to each other and looking in each other's eyes. Hearing each other's voice, seeing each other as they really look. Smelling each other! Ugh, that must have been hard!

Relationships weren't created through Instagram filters and selfies. When somebody lied, at least it was to your face! Now you can decide how you want to be seen by the world. You can get very friendly with strangers who will never know who you really are. You can be whomever you want to be. And you can be so many different people, you'll need to make sure that you don't forget your real self.

Unfortunately, in my case, even the people who are the closest to me and see me all the time, my parents and my brother, don't know who I really am.

And when they tell me that they love me, I think to myself: *How can you love someone you don't really know?*

THE VILLAIN

The first couple of airings of *The Rich and Beautiful Women of Beverly Hills* got low ratings. There were similar shows out there, and the reaction varied from 'so-so' to 'truly awful.' After the broadcast of the third episode, rumors spread that the show would soon be on the chopping block.

I didn't lose any sleep over it. Actually, I was pleased when I heard Libby discussing it with her fiancée, Lizzy, a columnist for *The Reporter*, while driving me to school in her Fiat 500. The reason Libby drove me to school every morning was because Mom and Dad couldn't get out of bed that early, and Carlos worked until very late. Libby was willing to come early and drop me off at school because she was an insomniac. She slept four hours a night, tops, and the pay was good.

While we rolled down the hill on the way to school one morning, Libby was explaining to Lizzy on the speakerphone that the network had told the producers to completely change the show, or go bust.

They were planning to get married in the summer, and most of the conversations in the car were about the wedding arrangements. It bored me to death, but this time the conversation was something else entirely. My earbuds were tucked into my ears, but the music was turned off and I heard every word they said.

"So what are they going to do?" Lizzy asked.

"I don't know. They need to find the 'X factor,'" Libby said.

"What's Luella's reaction?" asked Lizzy.

Libby glanced at me, but I pretended to mind my own business.

"She is in her usual panic mode. Hysterical, yelling, changing her mind every five minutes, going crazy and making everyone in the house miserable. I swear to God I wanted to smack her in the face yesterday. I thank Buddha, and you, darling, for keeping me calm and sane. Otherwise, who knows what I would've done?"

"I feel for you, honey," Lizzy said in a sweet voice. "You know what is really strange? She comes off on the show as a really nice person."

Libby let out a dismissive grunt. "She's acting nice, that's all."

She glanced at me again. I was sitting shotgun, but I was humming with my eyes closed.

"You see, in my opinion, that's the problem with the show. All four women are not really interesting to watch," Lizzy said. "They are almost too perfect. You need some intrigue, cheap sensation, something dramatic to make them stand out from the pack."

"I guess you're right. Perfect is boring," Libby agreed. "They're all too damn great. In the show, that is. In real life, they are four horrible bitches."

We arrived at school and I jumped out of the car.

Libby was a liar. While she was working for my mom and dad, she was leaking information and talking trash about Mom to her fiancée, who would use it later in her online column, which everyone in Hollywood reads. I hate the woman. In my opinion, it's she who needs a good smack in the face, not Mom.

Later that day, when I got home, I watched the show on my laptop. Although officially Mom had excused me from watching, because I was too young to watch, blah, blah, blah, she didn't ban it. She just suggested that it wasn't for me. Maybe she was embarrassed or afraid that I wouldn't like it. But she didn't tell me I couldn't watch it. It's like the warnings on cigarette packs. They tell you that you are going to die if you smoke, but it's your free choice if you choose to smoke, and no one but you is responsible if you die a horrible death. In our house, the rules were so flexible that, really, there were no rules. Every rule could be announced on a whim and changed on a whim, and no one cared. The one and only real rule has always been that I can do whatever the hell I want.

Instead of rules, my parents have suggestions. A couple of years ago, Dad told my brother Ian that he wouldn't recommend that he smoke marijuana because, in Dad's opinion, Ian was too young to do it. Dad admitted sheepishly that he had done it when he was sixteen years old, and Ian was already seventeen when they had the conversation.

"But I started when I was fifteen," Ian said, raising his eyes to the ceiling, making the point that Dad was clueless.

"Did your mother know?" Dad asked, trying to look shocked. Ian was Dad's son from his first wife, Melissa.

"I *will* tell her. Once she gets out of rehab," Ian told Dad firmly. "She is emotionally unstable now."

"It's very mature of you to make this observation," my father said. "I don't think you are old enough to smoke weed, but if you do it, I hope you do it responsibly."

Ian didn't answer. He didn't tell Dad that he was also seriously into alcohol. Being an alcoholic was something Dad dealt with his whole adult life, and Ian knew it would be too much of a burden for Dad if he'd told him that he was continuing the family tradition on the long and winding road into rehab. Anyhow, Dad didn't have a clue how to deal with Ian. He didn't know what to do because he was still learning to be a father. He told me that once, thinking his honesty was 'cool.' He was fifty-five with two kids that he brought into the world (who knows why?), and he was still trying to figure out parenting. And because he and Mom couldn't agree on anything, I was free as a bird. And Ian? He was trying to figure out his own life, tucked away in a small house in Silver Lake, doing drugs, drinking, and hanging out, which was his way of showing that he still had no idea what he wanted to do with his life. He told me that he wanted to be an artist. I guess he was trying to figure out what kind of an artist he wanted to become before starting to be one. He was only nineteen, and as long as Dad was paying his bills there was no immediate need on his part to come to a conclusive decision.

When I finished watching the show, I thought about what Lizzy had said and I knew she was right. I thought about the looming fate of the show. On one hand, it was a total embarrassment and I agreed that it should be wiped out completely. But on the other hand, the cancellation could bring a financial disaster to our family.

I hated the show, but I knew that we needed the money and that Mom would lose it completely if she failed again. And she and Dad would fight and their lives would be even more miserable. I knew I would survive, but I decided that I wanted to prevent my parents from suffering. I wanted to help them.

Later in the evening I went to Dad's office.

He was lying on the sofa, half dozing, and I woke him up. He was happy to see me, though he looked horrible.

"Hey, sweetie pie," he said. "What's up?"

"Nothing special. Working on your screenplay?" I asked.

He sighed. "I wish. In the last three weeks I haven't been able to come up with one word. I'm stuck."

I didn't want to dwell on it, because I knew he might cry. So I changed the subject.

"How's Mom doing in the show?"

"She's okay, I guess," he said.

"You haven't seen *The Reporter* today, have you?" I asked.

"What? Why?" he raised himself up from the sofa.

"The show tanked in the ratings. It might get cancelled."

"Oh my God," he said. He looked scared.

"Why do you think the show isn't working?" I asked. He was smart and knew a lot about showbiz.

"This reality garbage... to tell you the truth, it's beyond me. I don't get it and I wouldn't know how to fix it."

"Maybe the show is too safe," I said.

I took him by surprise. He looked at me with interest.

"What do you mean by that?"

"I hate this show as much as you do," I said. "But if you want a successful reality show, you need bad stuff to happen constantly. Remember, you told me that in all your movies the villain is the most exciting character, and without a great villain there is no conflict and no hero. In this show, all the women are nice and adorable. There's no villain, so it's too boring."

He smiled and nodded. "But this is a reality show," he said. "Not a work of fiction."

"But the people who watch it want the same stuff they get in any movie or drama. They want to hate, to love, to be excited. They don't care that it's a reality show."

He got it. He liked my pitch. "You are the smartest person in this family," he said. "You are a jewel!"

It felt good to see him relieved.

"So what will you do?" I asked.

"I'm not sure. Who can be the villain in this show?"

I didn't answer. I hoped he would come to the obvious conclusion without my assistance.

He looked at me, his eyes wide.

"No... No... You don't mean that?"

"Yes I do," I said calmly. "Someone needs to jump in and save the show."

"But Mom will be insulted!"

"Mom can play it perfectly. And she'll do anything to succeed."

"You're right," he said. "She will," he smiled.

"So?"

"I'm going to tell your mother to step it up a notch," he said and rose from his chair. "She should be the villain." He couldn't stop himself and mumbled as though I weren't in the room, "She is a natural."

He winked.

"Exactly," I said.

The concept of *The Rich and Beautiful Women of Beverly Hills* was pretty simple. In each episode, the audience got to watch a day in the life of four glamorous women. The women knew each other loosely in the beginning of the show, but as the show progressed from one mansion to another, following them in their daily routine, their relationships and roles were established.

If you are yawning while reading, don't feel bad.

My parents agreed that my father and I would be kept out of the show. So far it has worked out pretty well. When the film crew took over our house, I would be either in school or locked in my room upstairs. I didn't want to take any chances and get caught off guard and find myself on the show. But the producers were asking for more. The other women on the show brought in their husbands and kids. I knew it was only a matter of time until Dad and I would be kindly asked to take part.

Mom talked to Dad about it, asking him to change his mind, but his adamant answer was that he would do it over his dead body, to which Mom responded, "Your dead body won't do, darling. I need you alive and kicking."

But she couldn't make him change his mind.

After our conversation in his office, Dad went to speak with Mom in the kitchen while I hid behind the charming Aphrodite.

Mom was worried that the show would be cancelled. In the last few days since the story broke out, she had been on the brink of a nervous breakdown. When Mom was upset, she got friendly with her favorite medicine, Xanax. She popped the pills like they were popcorn, and it was okay because it was prescribed by Dr. Gold, her plastic 'magician.' Although Xanax isn't treated like cocaine or heroin, it can be just as addictive, and when consumed irresponsibly it can kill you.

Ian once joked to Mom that we had two law-abiding junkies in our family, Mom and Dad, and just one who broke the law.

He pointed to himself.

Mom didn't think it was funny.

But Mom couldn't live without her pills. They helped her deal with the tough periods in her life, which were most of the time.

Dad sat at the counter and had a strange look on his face. "You look sick," he said. "What's going on?"

"I had a terrible day, thank you," she said. "Those producers are so incompetent. They're killing the show."

"So I hear," Dad said. "Do you want to talk about it?"

"No!" Mom yelled. "My head is about to explode!"

Dad grabbed the Xanax bottle and put it in his pocket while Mom fixed herself a glass of Chardonnay.

"Be careful with the drinks," Dad warned her. "You took too many pills already."

"Look who's talking," she dismissed him bitterly. "Your breath is disgusting."

"I have an idea how we can save the show," he said.

She froze, her mouth wide open.

"Really?"

"Just listen," he said.

She nodded.

Without further ado he told her what I told him, that the show needed a villain. He didn't tell her it was my idea, because this is Hollywood, and in this town no one likes to give anybody else credit. As my father explained to me more than once, it comes with the territory. For example, he said, there were six different writers who rewrote his last screenplay. Dad was the first. He was fired and another writer was hired, and then it was his turn to be fired; he was followed by a third writer who came on board, and the process went on and on. But there were only three credits allowed when the film was completed, and Dad knew that a credit war would start before the film was released to determine who deserved the screenwriter credit.

So I wasn't totally surprised that Dad didn't give me credit. I was fine with it, because I wanted to be kept out of it anyway. Plus, it wasn't really my idea. I got it from Lizzy.

Because Mom was under the influence, she got calmer as she listened to Dad, who was making his point passionately. It was all about saving the show, he explained, and it was up to her to step up to the plate. She needed to create a fictional character, Dad argued.

"You need to become the villain," he said. "Everyone should hate you."

She didn't like it.

"Are you insane?" she asked.

"No," Dad said. "I'm being pragmatic. It's a role. It's not you. You'll act it."

She listened as he told her that she'd act so well that America would fall in love with her by hating her. Becoming the wicked, nasty woman in the show would make the show exciting to watch, he argued. Yet, she needed to do it without any advance warning, just do something nasty and shocking out of the blue in the next episode so the world would immediately buzz about it. And with a little help from TMZ and Twitter, the show would take off.

"But you don't think that I'm that kind of a woman, do you, darling?" Mom asked through the hazy cloud in which she was settling comfortably. "I would only be playing a character, right? It's not the real me."

She didn't say the obvious—that in a reality show the viewers perceive the people on the screen as the real them.

"Of course not, darling," Dad said, and put his hand on hers. "As I said, you'll be acting the villain. That's all."

A nice big white lie was shining in mid-air between them. "Okay," she agreed. "I'll do it. What's next?"

FROM LUELLA TO CRUELLA

The episode that changed the show and our lives forever was shot at our house. The four *RBW90210* stars got together for a segment called "Reality Check" where they told each other what they 'really' thought about their fellow stars. It was supposed to be the truth moment that led to passionate arguments mixed with tears and hugs.

This was the first time I was interested in watching the shoot. Being excused from school was easy. I told Mom I wasn't feeling well, and that was all I needed to stay home for the day.

But I didn't want the cast and crew to know who I was, so I decided to make it impossible for anyone to recognize me. At first everything I wore looked silly. Finally, I found a Catwoman mask in my closet that my dad bought me for Halloween a couple years ago. He thought it was cool, but I never wore it because I thought it was silly. Now it seemed like a good idea. I put it on and went down to the living room where the crew was getting ready to film. About a dozen people worked quietly. I walked out and saw a dozen more hovering in the street and back alley, where they parked their trucks and trailers. A policeman was hired to keep unannounced visitors off the premises, which was a joke, because on our street there is almost no foot traffic at all. The only passersby were tourists driven by tour guides who showed them the homes of celebrities.

Why people flocked to our neighborhood from the four corners of the world to have a peek at star homes is beyond me. They're probably the same people who watched *RBW90210* and other trashy shows on TV. Sometimes, when I saw them taking pictures, I wished I had a loudspeaker so I could yell at them to get a life.

I was wandering around the set for quite a while, and no one seemed to care. Normally I wouldn't expect people to notice me, but since I was wearing the Catwoman mask, I thought I'd get some funny looks. But no one even glanced at me or said a word. Yes, I know I said I didn't want to be noticed, but it makes you question what is wrong with these people.

It was mind blowing to see how long it took the film crew to get ready for shooting. I was sitting as close as possible to the director's monitor. His name was Bruce and he was about Dad's age, with salt and pepper hair and a quiet voice. A man and woman, who had the word 'producer' written all over their faces, stood nearby, texting feverishly.

At last, the four stars were ushered into our grand living room.

It was a parade of blond and blonder, although my mom insisted that she was the only natural blonde among them. Almost everything else on my mom's body was fake, so I understood why she was so proud to let everyone know that she was naturally blonde.

The four ladies, Julia, Megan, Kim, and my mom, were seated facing each other. The makeup and hair artists took care of the last looks, while Bruce gave his final instructions in a soft but assured voice. You might think that there was no script to the show, because the professionals called the reality show 'unscripted,' but this wasn't one hundred percent true. The show had writers who came up with plot ideas and wrote lines they wanted Mom and her co-stars to say because even in a stupid show you need someone who can write dumb lines that sound great.

The camera started to roll, the first Assistant Director called 'action,' and the conversation between the four ladies started. I swear, it was the most boring conversation I had ever listened to. They talked about all kind of things, but mainly about themselves and their petty relationships and their unimportant views about nothing. At a certain point they talked about who had the best taste in food. Not the food they were cooking, because they all stopped cooking a long time ago. They were talking about their favorite food and where they like to eat and who was the best chef in town and how much they were willing to spend for a 'to-die-for' meal in a fancy restaurant.

Then, as if Bruce read my mind, he asked, "Do you cook at home?" to which they all answered enthusiastically, "Yes!"

Apparently they cooked a lot and loved it, because cooking is a labor of love, and no matter how rich you are, cooking for the people you love is the most satisfying.

Obviously, my mom was lying about her cooking habits, and I bet that the others were too. Because as far as I can remember, I never saw my mom cook.

She always said she hated cooking and that she found the entire thing to be a huge waste of time.

But she didn't say that in front of the camera. She had to play her game so everyone could say, "Look at this rich, beautiful woman who cooks for her family although she can afford not to. What a classy lady!"

Bruce went on to ask what they liked to cook best.

"Just this morning I cooked a great breakfast for my daughter, Alexa," Mom said enthusiastically. "She loves my Eggs Benedict. It's her favorite before she goes to school."

I blushed behind my Catwoman mask. The last time Mom made me breakfast was never.

Eggs Benedict? I make myself granola and yogurt before I go to school, if I feel like having breakfast at all.

In the next few minutes, the four blondes boasted about their culinary achievements. I could hear Dad listening to this load of crap and thinking about Mom, "You, my dear, cook with your credit card."

But then came the moment when everything changed. The moment in a movie that Dad would call the *turning point*. They started to talk about real stuff. It was like adults playing truth or dare, but no matter what was asked, their answers were a bunch of baloney. You could tell they were all lying through their teeth.

Bruce had just yawned when my mom asked Megan out of the blue, using her sweetest and calmest voice, if it was true that she worked as a porn actress in her youth.

The next thirty seconds looked as though they were taken out of a cartoon where the character runs for his life and suddenly finds himself in mid-air, falling off a cliff, though his feet are still moving frantically. When Mom finished the question, the other three ladies started yelling at once so no one could hear what they were actually saying.

Bruce jumped as if he got shot in the arm.

"What did you just say, Luella?" he raised his voice above the chatter.

"I asked Megan," Mom said, and each word came out of her red lips loudly and clearly, "Is it true that she had starred in porn movies."

There was a moment of silence and the three women started yelling again as everyone else watched in awe.

"Wait," Bruce raised his voice, trying to control the commotion. "I need total silence on the set and I need Luella to ask the question again and Megan, please answer once Luella finishes the question."

"The answer is definitely no!" Megan yelled without waiting. She rose from the sofa trembling.

"Luella?" Bruce said.

"If she denies it, she's lying," Mom said. "Just Google it and find out."

Megan jumped on my mother, shrieking like a wounded animal. But Mom was ready. When Megan approached Mom, she slapped her in the face so hard that Megan stopped in her tracks and started to cry.

"Two and three, close up on Luella and Megan," Bruce whispered ecstatically.

Megan was shell-shocked. Her tears fell hard on our antique Persian carpet.

"Stop it! Just stop the cameras! I want to talk to my lawyer! I will sue you, you stupid bitch. And you," she pointed to Bruce. "And you!" she turned to the producers and then she stormed off the set.

Bruce hurried after her signaling to one of the cameramen to follow. "Luella," he said, "Go outside and try to confront her again."

Everyone rushed outside, with Mom up front leading the pack.

I must admit that what happened in our living room looked amazing in the show itself. The lighting, the editing, the music. Some of it was later rehearsed and reshot. But before it even hit the screen, the story and selected footage was leaked to the web by the show's publicist, Jeanine, a big woman with a beautiful smile who was an expert in turning an average fart into a record-breaking tweet.

Megan didn't sue anybody. She was given ample time to tell her side of the story in the show. Like how when she was a starving acting student she participated in a school project only to learn later that she was exploited by the director. Nobody really cared. Everyone was frantically trying to find the footage.

This moment of truth made Mom an instant star and quickly earned her the nickname Cruella.

She was furious at first but Dad swayed her not to fight it. She would become a brand, he claimed. It was good for the show and great for her.

"It's only a character you play," he said.

Mom justified her nickname in each of the following episodes. She always had a nasty card up her sleeve that she threw viciously at her co-stars. She didn't have to come up with it herself. The show's researchers gave her the ammunition by digging into the past of their own stars. The writers supplied her with punch lines. And she used her right hand a lot, slapping her co-stars in their beautiful faces when she didn't like their reactions. They created a vicious sound effect for her slaps. Bruce named it 'The Cruella effect.'

She became meaner in real life. It was as if the role she played exposed her true self or was taking over.

I wasn't sure. But it was pretty scary.

I never hated Mom. I sometimes even liked her. But she was becoming an easy target for hatred. Dad, who convinced her to take the role, was the first to realize that he had created a monster. He didn't tell me that, but his heavy drinking and dark moods told me he was starting to have second thoughts.

The network came up with a new show concept where my mom would be the only star. They ordered twelve episodes of the new show. She was still in the old show slapping her way left and right, but everyone's minds were on the new show. Mom's salary was quadrupled and, by the end of the first season, the network announced that *RBW90210* would be terminated to make way for an exciting new show.

The new show's name was—you probably already guessed it—*'Cruella.'*

WHAT'S YOUR SKELETON?

"Everyone has a skeleton in his or her closet," Grandpa Hilton told me over muffins at our usual spot, Joan's On Third.

"I don't," I said.

"You are too young, but you will, at one point or another," he promised.

"What's yours?" I asked.

"I have quite a few," he said smiling. "I am human after all. Aren't I, Joe?" he asked his nurse.

"If you say so, sir." Joe was looking at his phone, reading the latest update from his home in the Philippines. One of his cows had gotten sick and he was upset.

Joe had come all the way to America from the Philippines to take care of Grandpa Hilton. He couldn't make a living in his home country, so he had to leave behind a wife and three young kids in search of a decent job. Joe became his village's biggest cow owner thanks to Grandpa. He told Grandpa that with a small investment of two hundred dollars he could buy a cow that could be sold in a couple of years for six hundred bucks. Grandpa asked Joe if he would like to have him as a partner, and Joe happily agreed. Grandpa invested in ten young cows, two thousand dollars total, for fifty percent ownership. Every day they went over fresh videos of the herd sent to them by Joe's wife so they could monitor the progress of their investment. For Grandpa it was a drop in the bucket because he was a very wealthy man, but he liked his new venture very much. It kept him busy.

"After three divorces, I'm still okay financially," Grandpa told me. "But when I die, my money won't go to my kids, I can promise you that."

"Please don't die!" I felt a shiver in my spine.

Grandpa smiled. "Believe it or not, I am trying my best. You're the only one in the family that wants me to live forever. All the rest would love to see me dead and buried so they can put their sweaty hands on my money. But they'll be disappointed. I told your father already. Don't count on my money when I'm gone."

"Daddy doesn't want you dead," I protested.

"You *might* be right," he said. "But regardless, he would love to get a share of the pie. Did I mention to you that he stopped talking to me almost a year ago, because I told him that I'm not giving him money anymore? And Don and Mark are even worse."

Don and Mark were Dad's half-brothers. "Between you and me," Grandpa said, "I gave your dad enough. He needs to grow up and live according to his means. Is that too much to ask?"

I shrugged. All this money talk was beyond me.

Grandpa Hilton continued, "I was a billionaire and now, after all my divorce settlements, I'm a millionaire. But I worked hard all my life for every penny I earned."

"What did you do?"

"I was a mean son of a bitch," he laughed.

"And that made you a billionaire?" I asked.

"I was smart and hardworking. Some people are talented for business. It's a gift. And I was blessed with this gift. But I also had the killer instinct."

"But what about your skeletons?" I reminded him.

"I will tell you one day. Don't worry. And if I don't, you'll find them. Skeletons eventually make their way into the light of day," Grandpa said. "Now tell me about this show your mom is doing on TV. I hear that everyone loves to hate her and I must say I'm pleased because I really don't like your mother."

"I'm sorry," I said, and I meant it.

Mom's name from her previous marriage was Luella Walker and this was the name she used on the show. This is why no one knew that I was the daughter of the most hated woman on TV and my zero social life went on uninterrupted with no fuss whatsoever. The problem was that the news media wanted to write about Mom's life and it was hard to keep me out of it, although to her credit, she tried pretty hard to protect me. It became a bigger issue when Mom was starring in her own show. The network demanded that the entire family take part in it. Ian lived in Silver Lake and no one really looked at him seriously as a candidate, so only Dad and I were targeted.

One Friday evening we went to The Ivy, Mom's favorite hangout, to celebrate the successful launch of *Cruella*. Two episodes had already aired and the show was doing much better than *RBW90210*. Dad and I showed up first and Mom arrived a few minutes later. We could see the paparazzi hovering on the sidewalk, buzzing around her. When she came into the restaurant and took her seat, she sighed and said, "I crave to be left alone. It's a madhouse."

I stared at her in disbelief.

"You love the attention," Dad said. "We get it."

"Do I hear a hint of jealousy?" she gave him her destroying look.

He hid behind the menu and chose not to respond.

Ian showed up and took his seat. "Sorry I'm late," he mumbled. He looked as if he had slept in the same clothes the entire week, but no one really seemed to care.

My favorite dish was the *pizza Margherita*. Ian said that he knew people who could live two days off the price of the pizza.

"You don't go to an expensive restaurant for a bargain," Mom said with a dismissive look. She thought Ian was a useless bum.

We looked at each other trying to figure out what she just said.

My father grimaced. "You mean restaurants that cater to rich people ought to have high prices?"

"Sure," Mom said with a smile reserved for slow thinkers. "If they charge low prices, everyone will show up at the door and the place will lose its allure."

"So a restaurant for the rich and famous can't have reasonable prices," Ian concluded. "It's not because they want to rip people off. It's just to make it harder for the average Joe to enjoy their exquisite food."

"Indeed," my mom said. "And 'rip-off' is a relative term that is commonly used by people who have no class," she smiled, as if she had just come up with the theory of relativity.

"Or they're not stupid enough to pay a ton of money for pizza," I said. But I knew I was a bit of a hypocrite, because I wanted my *Margherita* now and I didn't care about the cost.

"It's time to order. I'm starving," Dad said.

The conversation during dinner became heated as Mom raised the issue of Dad and I joining the show.

"No way," Dad said.

"I want to do it," Ian said.

"Do you?" Mom said in her most disparaging tone.

"Why not?" he said. "I'll attract the youth demographic. I'll bring the Millennials to watch your show."

"You'll embarrass yourself," Mom said. "America will laugh at you. Don't even think about it."

He stared at her and I saw the rage in his eyes. "You are old, Cruella. Face it."

She looked at her hands as if she were about to scratch his face with her fingernails ."How would you do it? You're stoned most of the time," she said, and her eyes pierced him with contempt.

"Exactly," Ian said cheerfully. "That's the hook! That's where I'll connect with the audience."

Mom grunted and waved her hand in dismissal. Dad felt it would be better to continue the fight at home.

"Okay, just calm down everyone," he said sheepishly. "We'll go home and talk it over. But first have a look at the dessert. Right, Alexa?"

I just nodded.

Carlos got us back home safely with the Lexus SUV and arrangements were made for Mom's Tesla to be driven home because she was too drunk to drive.

When we got home, we sat around the kitchen table and Gabby made tea and coffee for the adults and chocolate milk for me.

"You don't want to do the show, I get that," Mom said to my dad. "But what about Alexa?" She was a bit less feisty, but she couldn't let go.

"Alexa is not going to be on the show," Dad raised his voice. "She is too young for that kind of exposure!"

"Let's ask the girl," Mom said in her most flattering voice.

"I'm in," I said.

"Oh, no!" Dad said in despair.

"Oh, yes!" Mom said in delight.

"On one condition," I interjected. "It won't be me. I want to wear a mask."

"A mask?" Everyone looked at me as if I had just landed from Mars.

"Yeah. A Catwoman mask. And my name on the show will be Daffodil, not Alexa."

Ian looked at me, pleased, "You are something else, Alexa. Sorry... Daffodil."

"But why?" Mom looked lost. "It's a reality show. They want to see my daughter. Not a masked girl with a foolish name."

I knew it was coming, so I told myself to stay calm. "I need the mask because I don't want to be identified. And no one should know I'm your daughter either. And the name? I don't think it's foolish to have a stage name. And it has a meaning, at least for me."

Dad was smiling.

"Why a stage name?" Mom asked. "It is you America wants to see!"

"*Your* name on the show isn't your real name," I said, staring at her.

"Luella Walker is my name from my previous marriage," Mom insisted, and blushed.

"Yes, Mom, but your given name is not Luella. It's Jane," I said.

A moment of silence took over as I dropped my bomb.

"But how...?" Mom said. She looked crushed, but I didn't feel anything. No sympathy and no anger. Just 100% pure organic nothing.

"It's all over the web," I said. "With your fake resume and all. It went viral while we were at The Ivy."

It was Ian who was the first to jump and catch Mom in his arms when she collapsed. He played football in high school, and it came in handy.

A PINK LIE

The ratings of *Cruella* accelerated after Mom's fake resume story was discussed and tossed around like a used tissue. No one cared that she lied on her resume. She wasn't a Princeton graduate as she declared. So what? The truth was, she dropped out after a year in a community college. She didn't win the 2002 Young Interior Designer award. This award didn't even exist. And she never worked with the world-renowned architect, Frank Gehry, on any of his famous projects. The scandal actually made her more popular because she didn't let it destroy her. She fought back by saying that she had to do it in order to get to where she was now. Which wasn't a lie. She just projected what she could have done if she were given the opportunity. She argued that the stuff she made up on her resume helped her grow and fulfill her potential. So no one should condemn her for doing what she had to do.

Her Facebook page ballooned with likes. People liked her audacity. It paved the way for millions of other people who could, with a few keystrokes, create a great resume for themselves and feel good about it.

Cruella became a star and an American role model. Mom was busier than ever, and when I saw her briefly at home, she seemed as if she was wrapped in the foggy cloud called success. She looked glitzier, happier, and out of reach. She wasn't paying attention to anyone. She wasn't really listening or even looking at me when we saw each other briefly. Jane was looking at Luella in awe, and Luella was worshiping *Cruella,* and there was nothing left for the people around her. Dad, me, Ian, and all the rest.

Mom tweeted that she wanted to get away to an exotic destination, as far away as possible, where we could be a family again without the commotion, the noise, and the paparazzi. She needed some time off, she said, thousands of miles away from LA, with white beaches and palm trees that moved softly in the wind.

"Let's go to Costa Rica," Dad texted, and we all met in the kitchen to discuss the details.

"Great," she said, and her eyes lit up. "But how do we get there?"

Dad wasn't sure what she was asking.

"We can't do it on a commercial flight," she said. "Not anymore."

"We don't have that kind of money," Dad said. "The days we could afford a private jet are over."

She gave him a look as though he was the stingiest person on earth.

"Okay, fine. We can't fly to Costa Rica then. But I'm not giving up on my getaway fantasy," she announced.

She booked a couple of suites in the Bel-Air Hotel for the weekend. It was a ten-minute drive from home, which makes perfect sense if you want to get far away from LA without the hard part of getting there.

The first day was great. We sunbathed by the pool and no one seemed to care who we were. Dad read a book, Mom just chilled with her eyes closed, and I hovered around. But Mom couldn't really detach from her show. Apparently, someone came up with the idea that Mom and Dad should renew their wedding vows in front of the camera.

Mom thought it was the best idea she had heard in a long time. "It will show the world how strong our relationship is," Mom told him. "We'll renew our vows in front of America."

Dad looked terrified. "Why do we have to do it all over again? We just did it not too long ago."

"Thirteen years ago," Mom said softly. "It seems like yesterday to me."

"It might be premature," Dad said sarcastically. "We need to wait a few more years to see if our marriage is worth another celebration."

"We should stay present and follow our heart," Mom said. She moved from her pool chair to sit on the edge of his chair and started stroking his shoulder.

"I didn't agree to be on the show anyway," Dad said in a weak voice. He was frozen, as if her hand was a reptile crawling on his shoulder.

Don't be such a coward, I prayed. Stand up to her!

But she was pressing harder. "Being on the show will do wonders for your career," she said. "We need to remind the world what a great writer you are!"

Dad didn't answer. Most of the time he just shrugged, which is what he did this time too. I was afraid he would surrender and do what Mom wanted him to do.

He mumbled that he was going to the bar for a beer and disappeared quickly. He needed his medicine to stay defiant.

Mom wasn't happy. I suspected the whole getaway thing was to corner my poor dad and make him agree. She turned her attention to me, but I rushed to the pool and dove in. Under the water I was safely out of her reach.

People are desperate to tie the knot. We are programmed to get ready for the day when we will fulfill our destiny and walk down the aisle. Especially girls.

Don't count on me to go down that road. Judging from how many people around me are divorced, and quite a few more than once, I decided that the goal of marrying someone and bringing children into the world is grossly overrated.

I'm eleven years old, and it is clear to me that I'm not going to marry anyone ever. It's just a huge waste of time in my opinion. Why people do it over and over again is beyond me. Happily ever after? Are you kidding me? Most of the married couples I know are miserable to the core, starting with my parents.

The problem lies in the fairy tales we are fed right from the start. We are under attack from movies and books and songs, millions of them that promote love and its end result, marriage as the ultimate goal, with the promise of living happily ever after while bringing into the world another generation that will be fed with the same horse manure.

This is what I call a *pink lie. Get your own Prince Charming on a white horse and you'll live happily ever after.*

Sooner or later this world will come to an end. There is no way around it. But even during the universe's last minutes, people will be planning their weddings. The highest point of their life from which everything else goes downhill.

You might think I'm weird. In school they *definitely* think I'm weird. I'm not much of a talker, I don't look for company, I mind my own business. And I hope each day that school will end soon so I can be back in my room doing what I like to do: reading, listening to music, watching the world fall apart, and my family get crazier.

My parents got nervous when they realized I was a loner. So they made me go to a shrink, a nice lady in a lavishly decorated office down on South Beverly Drive. At the first appointment, I sat there trying to answer her questions politely just to get it over with. But when she told me that she would see me next week, I said, "I don't think so."

"Why?" she asked and didn't look surprised.

"I want to stay as I am," I said. "I don't want to talk to you or anyone about myself and I feel pretty damn good about myself. So why waste our time and my parents' money?"

I don't remember what she said because I didn't listen. It happens all the time. I see people's mouths move, but the voices I hear are mine.

I hate social media and I don't text like crazy all day long like everyone around me. Grandpa Hilton told me that he likens the smartphone to a pacifier. Anyway, most of the stuff people post online exposes how boring they really are.

People are boring. Period. They're scared of shutting up and listening to their inner voices because they might go nuts. But for me, my inner voices are my best friends and my mind is the place where I live happily. And guess what? In my solitude I can listen to myself and to others.

If I care to.

ROBERTA

You can hardly see homeless people in our lovely city, because when they do appear in our streets, the police are quick to show them the way out. That's why the appearance of a lady in an old army jacket, pushing a supermarket cart up the hill, caught my attention. It was one of those rare occasions when Mom picked me up after school. She had a production meeting nearby and said she wanted to talk to me about my upcoming appearance on the show.

It was totally unexpected when Mom let out a cry and stomped on the brakes of the Tesla.

"What?" I asked.

"Nothing. Just sit tight," she ordered, and jumped out of the car.

I saw her talking to the homeless woman. They exchanged a few words and then suddenly something crazy happened.

Mom and the woman hugged.

Mom came back to the car and I opened the window.

"I need money. Do you have some cash?" she asked me in a shaky voice.

"I have eight bucks," I said. "Why? Who is that woman?"

"She's someone," my mom said in a rush. "I'll tell you later."

She took the money from me and went back to the woman. They talked and I saw the homeless lady refuse to take the money. She nodded 'no' a couple of times.

Mom came back to the car. She looked lost.

"She wants to come stay with us. I don't know what to do. I told her to take the money for now and I'll meet her later and give her some more. She says no. She doesn't need money. She wants proper hospitality."

"Who is she, Mom?"

She looked at me and I saw the worry in her eyes. "It's your aunt. My sister Roberta."

I couldn't believe it.

"You never told me you had a sister," I said.

"I planned to someday," Mom said in a muffled voice. "But what do we do now?"

"Well, there is only one answer. We take her home," I said.

"How? She has all this disgusting garbage with her!" Mom said in panic.

"Tell her to leave it here and we'll send Carlos to pick it up."

Mom nodded. She went back to her sister and they talked some more.

"What?" I said, when she entered the car.

"She said no. She can't leave her valuables unattended," Mom said, in a 'can you believe it?' tone. "She'll arrive soon. It's only an hour's walk. That's how she planned it." Mom looked agitated. "You can't change her mind. She is the most stubborn person I've ever known."

"She seems fine to me." I couldn't take my eyes off the woman who had now restarted her slow pace up the hill.

Mom turned on the car and we left Roberta behind. I looked back at her until she disappeared from view.

"How come she is homeless?" I asked.

"She isn't your run-of-the-mill homeless person," Mom said.

"I don't get it."

"Never mind, it's a long story," Mom said nervously.

Roberta's arrival was greeted with very little surprise. The staff already knew that we were somewhat crazy (Dad called us eccentric) and everyone minded their own business. Dad behaved as though Roberta was a breath of fresh air, and Mom decided that the best way to deal with her was to pretend that she wasn't there.

We quickly learned that Roberta was unpredictable. Mom gave her a beautiful room overlooking the hills, but she left it in the middle of the night and settled in the gazebo by the swimming pool where she created a makeshift bedroom for herself. She slept in a hammock that no one ever used because we barely spent time by the pool. Later, she said that she hated the indoors and that the gazebo was perfectly fine.

The next morning, as I was getting ready for school, I saw Roberta from the kitchen window getting out of the pool, naked.

Dad was leaving his shack to grab his hangover buster, a triple espresso, black, no sugar, and bumped into her. I laughed my head off when I saw the look on his face. He rushed into the house and brought her a towel, but she refused it with a laugh and he immediately disappeared into his hideout.

I went out to have a closer look and saw Mom watching from her second-floor bedroom in horror.

"What's going on out there?" she yelled.

She was getting ready for a shooting day, her face covered with a facial mask. She quickly rushed out, trying to talk some reason into Roberta, who was diving into the pool and popping out occasionally, like a dolphin.

In seconds, the two sisters began yelling at each other, and then Roberta did the unthinkable and pulled Mom, who was dressed in her best clothes, into the pool. The screams brought the entire house out.

"Did you see it?" I asked Gabby, who ran into the backyard, her eyes wide with astonishment. She went back inside and brought Mom a bathrobe and towel. Mom got out of the pool wailing, and ran back into the house.

Roberta popped out and let out a laugh. "That was fun!" she cried out.

A few minutes later in the kitchen, Gabby said. "Your aunt is loco, she hurt your Mom and this is not nice because Luella was very nice to her."

"Why?"

"She didn't kick her out, right? Your mom has a good heart."

Mom wasn't getting a lot of compliments about her good heart lately. I thought about what Gabby said and I liked it.

"Would you let her stay?"

Gabby smiled. "Me? No! I'd kick her out of my house, even if she were my sister," she exclaimed.

"But you are a kind person."

"Thank you, Alexa. I try my best. But at my house, nobody walks around naked," she said and blushed.

"I think my mom let Roberta stay because we're all just as crazy as she is," I said thoughtfully.

Gabby smiled at me sadly. I guess she agreed.

Mom didn't kick Roberta out, and I savored every minute with my aunt. I spent hours in her makeshift bedroom outside under the gazebo.

I asked her why she'd never visited us before.

"Because Jane and I aren't very close," she called Mom by her real name.

"Mom never told me about you," I said.

"We never got along," Roberta said. "There's a gap of eight years between the two of us and I took off early. When I was sixteen, I ran away and your mom grew up without her older sister. There's a lingering grudge because she was left to deal with our parents, your grandparents, who were hard on her, and she felt that I had deserted her. I suppose we don't have much in common," she laughed, "except a deep disdain toward our parents."

Roberta was prettier than Mom, but her long hair was grey, her face wrinkled, and she looked way older. I had no doubt Dr. Gold's magic wand could turn her into a star.

"But why are you homeless?"

Roberta looked at me with her piercing gaze and smiled. "I'm not really homeless. I'm more like a self-appointed homeless ranger. When I live in the streets I have a purpose. I live among homeless people, I talk to them, get to know them, and when they need help, I'm there for them."

"But why?"

"When you are among them, it's easier to see and feel things in a different way," she said.

"Are you broke?"

"Not broke. Just broken. But I'm trying to fix myself. Make something meaningful out of the pieces."

She confused me. I saw in her eyes that she knew I didn't quite get what she was talking about. There was something she wasn't telling me.

I asked her if I could record her on my iPhone and she didn't mind. I think she actually liked it.

She told me stories about my grandpa and grandma who died long ago. She told me stories about Mom when she was a child, before Roberta ran away. She laughed a lot and every once in a while she jumped naked into the pool. When she smoked weed she asked me to kindly leave, and often, when I checked how she was doing, I found her asleep in the hammock. I looked at her face and I knew she was dreaming because she was smiling.

COLORFUL LIES

Roberta was the smartest person I ever met. She asked me questions and I told her everything, and I made her laugh. A few times she started tearing up while I was talking, because she said I was opening a faucet of emotions inside her. But I liked it best when she told me stuff. She made me think. She knew so much and she came up with a lot of wise ideas about life.

She said she had made dumb decisions in her life, and the hardest thing was to accept them. But what was even harder was to accept herself.

"You are the wisest person I have ever met," I protested.

"Thank you, honey. That is a great compliment. I'm a work in progress," she said smiling.

"When will the work be done?" I asked.

"Never," she said, and burst out laughing.

One morning, after staying with us for a couple of weeks, she was gone. She didn't bother to say goodbye. The only thing she left me was an old Joni Mitchell vinyl album, *Blue,* with a note that said, "I know you are going to love it."

I pushed the silly album aside. I hated her so much.

I locked myself in my room until late that night. Mom finally knocked on the door and asked me to let her in.

She hugged me. "I know you are sad. I'm also sad. But that's Roberta. Always unpredictable."

"Where is she now?" I asked.

"I don't know. She might be somewhere downtown, or she could have gone someplace else. I'm not sure where she lives because she never told me. She wants to be left alone, and we have to respect that."

When Mom was gone I thought about it and wanted to smack myself in the face. I never asked Roberta two simple questions: where do you live and what do you do when you aren't on the streets?

DAFFODIL

The third broadcast of *Cruella* was a bit of a disappointment. Each episode was about Mom being a *normal* Beverly Hills mother and wife turned into a national celebrity turned into a normal 90210 woman again.

The villain was tamed and it was boring, so the viewers began turning their backs on the show.

"I hate these traitors, deserters, and spineless fans!" Mom said bitterly. "Is it so hard to love me?" she asked. "What did I do to them to deserve this?" she yelled. "I'm the same old me!"

The ratings that had previously skyrocketed were now just okay, and most of the reviews were awful. Only one review seemed great, but not for long—just until Mom read it from top to bottom. The headline in the *LA Times* TV section was "A Star Is Born," but after her initial joy, she realized that it wasn't attributed to her.

The critic wrote that the show was horrendous. The only ray of light was the masked girl, Daffodil, though no one exactly knew what her relation to Cruella was. He went on to say that Daffodil stole the show and that she was the only one who could save it.

"She is a ray of light, a stroke of genius in what is otherwise a dull, boring show," the critic concluded.

Luckily, the day that review came out, while Mom cussed and yelled and threw stuff in the kitchen, I was in school. I didn't even watch the show. I never would have watched that garbage voluntarily anyway.

Libby picked me up that afternoon. Dad wanted her to give me a heads up in case Mom went into a tantrum when I got back.

"I don't get it," I told Libby. "I didn't even do anything in the show."

"Your segment made the show. They zoomed in on you for a few minutes and that was that," Libby said with pride.

I shrugged.

"Why Daffodil?" she asked. "What a cool name!"

"Narcissus," I said.

"Doesn't ring a bell," Libby said. "A rapper?"

"Google him," I said.

She wasn't really listening. She was beaming with pride. "Didn't you realize how funny you were when you were on?"

"No," I said, "I was answering Bruce's questions very seriously."

She laughed again.

"You are a star, Alexa."

"You mean Daffodil is a star," I corrected her.

"Yes, Daffodil. Sorry," she glanced at me with a smirk.

Mom was in her bedroom, the curtains were drawn, and a sufficient dose of pills were in her belly to remove all the negative thoughts from her head.

I stood at the door, a safe distance away, "What's going on, Mom?"

"It's my usual migraine," she said faintly. "I'll be okay soon. Come give me a hug."

I went to her bedside but she was too weak to embrace me. I kissed her cheek and took her hand.

Her eyes were shut. She looked as pale as a sheet.

She didn't say anything. I waited for a long minute and didn't know what to do. I didn't like these moments. It was totally awkward and I wanted her to say something, but her hand still gripped mine, so I waited until I heard the steady rhythm of her breath and saw that she had fallen asleep. I released her grip and went quietly out.

Chilling in my room, I tried to think everything over. Roberta told me that Mom was giving me too much freedom. I was left alone to make my own choices, and when Mom was helpless it felt like she was the child and I was the adult. I knew Mom was telling me something by collapsing into her migraine. And it had to do with my being on the show.

Against my own rules of never watching *Cruella,* I checked online and found my clip on YouTube. Since last night it received two hundred thousand views. I took a deep breath and watched it. It was horrible. I looked like a bad joke. Why did people like it? Maybe because I was a buffoon?

Voice (while the camera bumps into me in the corridor): "She is a mysterious member of the family. She walks around the house in a Catwoman mask."

A cut to Mom in close-up saying: "My life in the limelight is my business, but other people in my house are wary about their privacy, which I perfectly understand. They don't have to be exposed and pay the price a celebrity of my caliber has to pay."

Cut to me.

Voice (Bruce's): Nice to meet you.

Daffodil: Not so nice to meet you.

Voice: Why?

Daffodil: You are an annoying white male who makes a living by snooping into other people's lives. You should be arrested for invasion of privacy.

(A big laugh comes from the people behind the camera as it follows Daffodil to her room. She turns around.)

Daffodil: "Stop following me or I'll call the police."

Voice: "Is this your room?"

Daffodil: "It's none of your business. It's off limits for you and your kind."

Voice: "What is my kind?"

Daffodil: "You are a leach, sucking on other people's lives."

Voice: "It's a show and you are part of it. I'm only doing my job."

Daffodil: "I'm not a part of your show. And anyway, it's a garbage show. The people who watch this show are garbage viewers. Go get a life, you people! Watching the so-called rich and famous won't get you anywhere."

Voice: "It's entertainment."

Daffodil: "Yeah, for people with no brains. It's all a lie, and you are spreading the lie. Now, excuse me. I have homework to do."

At that point I opened the door to my room and slammed it in their faces.

The camera stayed on the door.

Voice: "Wait! What is your name, Catwoman?"

I shouted from behind the door: "Daffodil. My name is Daffodil."

I watched it twice. It was horrific. I hated my squeaky voice. The best part of it was when they went to commercial break.

I read some of the comments. Most thought it was hilarious and some were offended. But for the most part, people sided with me.

"A brilliant idea," wrote one of the bloggers. "The best thing that happened to any reality show in recent memory. A bold move."

A bold move?

I needed to talk to Roberta. It was getting out of control and I needed someone to help me figure it out.

I looked out the window. The gazebo was as beautiful as ever. The empty hammock didn't move. I felt a pinching pain. Why did she have to leave?

A PURPLE LIE
AND A BLACK LIE

Getting used to my new status was easier than I thought. At first people asked me in school if I was Daffodil, and I said with a disgusted look, "Are you crazy?" I wanted them to believe that I hated this creature. To those who wouldn't let go, I said that I was not supposed to tell them because it was highly confidential, but if they kept their mouth shut I would. "The girl with the funny mask on the show is a child actor," I lied. "She was hired by the show because my mom didn't want me to get involved, and everything she said was written for her."

It rang so true to my listeners that it struck me that no one in my class believed I was able to be Daffodil, and believe it or not, it hurt for a nanosecond.

But it worked. People left me alone. Or so I thought.

At home, things almost went back to normal. Mom realized that she was still the star of the show. In every episode, I performed my schtick—delivering a few minutes of rant—and everyone thought that Daffodil was a genius. Still, Mom was on the screen most of the time. My presence attracted viewers and made the show a hit, and she liked that. But deep down I knew she couldn't forgive me because it was I, and not she, who was making it a hit.

"Honestly," she said to me, "I love your segment. It makes the show so much better."

'Honestly.' I hate the word 'honestly.' In my opinion, if a person uses that word at least three times a day he must be a certified liar. Mom uses it a lot, but she isn't only a certified liar. She is more than that. She believes that everything she says is true. She will prove it to you if you doubt her.

And even more outrageously annoying, she could look at the facts presented to her and say, without blinking, that they are all lies and believe herself wholeheartedly.

I had to come up with a fitting color for Mom's kind of lying. Black was appropriate, because it was her favorite color. *A black lie is one you tell yourself and believe—and in your mind there is no boundary between the truth and the lies.*

Honestly, I was okay with the show. And I promise not to use this word again, so you'll know that I'm telling the truth. After all, Daffodil wasn't me. I was Alexa. Daffodil was an invented character. I made her up and people had their own interpretations. But the more I thought about it, I had to admit that I was twisting the truth a bit. Not lying but not telling the truth either.

I call it a *purple lie.*

Why purple? Because I love the color purple, and if there is a color that describes what I was doing it should be purple.

I wasn't telling the whole truth. Honestly (oops!), I didn't see a way out. Because the only way out was quitting the show, and I realized that I didn't want to quit. I liked my little game in front of the camera, talking to three million viewers who watched the show religiously and wanted to hear every word I had to say.

I promised myself that I wouldn't watch the show and that I wouldn't read the comments and discussions on social media. But there were a few cracks in the bubble I created for myself. Libby quoted things that people were saying about me. She asked me about stuff that I had said.

"There's nothing special about it," I said.

"Well," she said, "The things you say are smart. It's like someone wrote it for you."

I smiled and didn't say a word.

"I know that you are exceptionally smart, but still… you are only eleven!"

"I'm actually almost twelve," I said, and started to feel a little knot building in my belly.

She had good instincts and she was nosy.

"I read what smart people say and I give it a twist," I said.

"So you quote other people?"

"Sort of. But it comes out differently. I use other ideas and mix them with my own."

My cheeks were red, but I needed to get her off my back.

She liked it. "Very smart! All the greatest people do it. They tap into someone else's stuff and take it to the next level. Steve Jobs is a good example, so you are in good company." She looked at me in admiration.

"What about the Arctic Monkeys?" I asked. They were my favorite band.

"Don't know. Never been to the North Pole," Libby said. I think she was serious because she didn't wink.

Everyone said that the fourth episode was the best by far.

Voice: "Can you name the ten best things on your wish list?"

Daffodil: "Why?"

Voice: "People would like to know you better. It's interesting."

Daffodil: "No. I think people want to know what I like because I'm on TV and they want to like it too, because they want to be like me. You can be the stupidest person ever, but people want to know what you think and what you like because you're famous. And what you like becomes important to them and they start to like it too."

Voice: "Why?"

Daffodil: "That's a question you should ask people who are smarter than me. I'm only eleven years old. But don't ask the viewers of this show. They are just plain dumb because they waste their time watching it. I apologize to anyone whom I am insulting, but in all frankness you truly deserve it. You need to wake up, people, turn off the TV, and do something with your lives!"

Voice: "What's wrong with good entertainment?"

Daffodil: "Nothing. But everything is wrong with this show. Dead people watching how dead people live, and they pass time in order not to think about their imminent deaths. The real one."

Voice: "Who's dead?"

Daffodil: "You, me, everyone. We breathe and talk and pretend we are alive, but we are dead."

Voice: "This is some bleak stuff for an eleven year old."

Daffodil: "Yeah, well, I'm almost twelve. Are you worried that your audience will switch channels and watch something else?"

Voice: "No. I think people are intrigued by you."

Daffodil: "I'm sorry anyway. Please make it short, I got to go."

Voice: "Let's go back to your list. What are the best ten things on your wish list?"

Daffodil: "Number one on my list is to be left alone. Number two is being by myself and not having to answer silly questions. The rest is totally private."

Voice: "Why do you want to be left alone?"

Daffodil: "Because that is how I feel good. That is when I am most myself."

Voice: "And who are you?"

Daffodil: "I don't know yet. I am too young to know. I'm a work in progress."

THE KNIGHT

I was leafing through my text messages when my eyes fell on a message from Justin the Knight. The kid who befriended me on Facebook and whose every move I followed ever since. It felt unreal so I read it six times before I concluded that even if it was fake, it looked authentic.

"Hey. Like to chat with you. I think I saw you on TV. Meow. Haha. Justin."

I took my fingers off the phone to fight my urge to respond now. I was so excited that I was afraid I'd write stupid stuff and ruin everything. I gave myself twenty-four hours to think it over before I responded. First off, he was two years older than me. I needed to behave like a grownup. A grownup child, not the grownup adults who were hanging around with me. The problem was, I was too excited to think of something really good. And I couldn't wait twenty-four hours either, because I was too excited period. I was a mess, and when you are a mess you do stuff you regret later. But you still do it.

The pressure on my fingertips was unbearable. "Sure. What do you want to chat about?" I wrote and waited for a long five seconds before I hit send.

Two seconds later the answer came, like a lightning bolt on a mid-summer day:

"Nothing. LOL!"

I felt sick to my stomach. Was he trying to mess with me?

"Are you a moron?"

"Nope! Are you?"

At least he didn't LOL again.

I hate LOL. I already told you it's a 'no-fly-zone' expression.

"No, but I feel that this chat will make me feel like one," I wrote fast and hit back.

"LOL. You are funny!"

"So?"

"Sorry. Need to go. Can we chat later?"

"Why?"

"Because you are funny!"

"But you aren't."

"LOL!!!"

And he was gone.

I hated it. I wanted to continue chatting and show him how much I despised him. But I couldn't. Now I had to wait until his next text and it was too painful to just sit and wait. And wait for what? He made me anxious and restless *and* he had ruined my day. I looked at his pictures for the millionth time and I knew that even if he wasn't really what I hoped he was, I wanted it to last. And the funny thing about it—which wasn't funny at all—was that this feeling was pretty bad. I felt sick. And I wondered why. And I wondered what I should do to feel better. But I had no idea. I was dying to talk to Roberta. I needed her soothing words. She was the smartest person I have ever met. The other person was Grandpa Hilton, but being a man, I wasn't sure I could tell him everything. It took me an hour to realize I couldn't hold it anymore.

I called Grandpa Hilton and heard some pretty loud noises in the background.

"Who is it?" he demanded.

"It's me, Alexa."

"Alexa? Where are you, sweetie?" his voice lightened up.

"At home," I said.

"I meant to call you," Grandpa said, "But I forgot. I'm at the airport with Joe. We are flying to the Philippines."

"Why?" That was a shocker.

"To take a look at our cows. I want to see my investment with my own eyes."

"When are you coming back?" I asked.

"In a couple of weeks. I'll meet you then."

"Is it a long flight?"

"Yeah, but we're flying first class, so I'll be fine. Take care, kiddo!"

"Have a safe trip, Grandpa. I'll miss you," I said but he had already hung up. My heart ached because my only friend in the entire universe was going away and I felt scared and abandoned. I also felt angry with him, because Grandpa hadn't bothered to tell me that he planned on going away. He was acting selfish, but I couldn't do anything about it, could I?

I got a terrible headache. My huge room shrunk and the only bright spots were my bed, my pillow, and the window overlooking the yard. I was lying on the bed with my eyes closed for a long time and then it hit me that if I didn't want to feel sorry and helpless I needed to do something. Roberta told me that it was my choice to act and change things. It was weird coming from a person who chose to be homeless. She read my mind and said that everything, as long as it's your own free will and you don't hurt anyone, is nobody's business.

So I took my smartphone and texted him fast as if I didn't want to be stopped. "I will send my driver to pick you up so we can meet. I would like to see if you are as smart as you think you are."

Ten minutes later, he answered. "You're badass! I'll wait for your driver at Chipotle on South Beverly Drive."

"What time?"

"Now. I'm there already."

"Okay."

Carlos was in the kitchen drinking his coffee and looking bored when I burst in breathless and asked him if he could get down to South Beverly and pick up someone.

"I was half asleep," he said. "Needed some action. Are you coming?"

"No," I said, my heart beating fast, "Just bring him here."

"It's a boy?" He looked surprised or did I imagine that?

Anyhow, I blushed. Then I nodded.

"Okay." He rose from the kitchen counter, coffee still in hand, and yawned.

I told him to text me when he got to the restaurant so I could tell Justin to step outside.

I texted Justin that Carlos, driving a black Lexus SUV, would arrive in ten minutes or so.

"No problem," was the answer.

I looked blankly at my iPhone, already regretting the whole thing.

What would Roberta say about this? I imagined she would approve. I was proactive. This is a word she liked a lot.

She would say, 'Enjoy the moment.' I could hear her raspy voice in my ears.

"Be you," she would have said too.

But who am I?

Twenty minutes later, I heard the car pull into the driveway. I thought I should go down and greet my guest.

This is how you do it, right?

I went down the stairs slowly. Carlos ushered my guest inside. He stood in the large hallway under the grand chandelier, looking around. I stopped for a second, my heart beating hard.

Then he looked up and his eyes met mine.

It felt wrong. He smiled, but I didn't smile back.

This boy was not Justin the Knight. He wasn't the one I knew so well from his gazillion selfies.

This was some chubby kid, with curly hair and a round face.

And he was short.

I moved down two steps. From a safe distance, I said a weak "Hi," while Carlos was watching us in amusement.

"Hi," the boy said. "You're not Justin," I said.

"No," he said, "I'm Guy. Guy Green. Justin couldn't come."

What? Someone was pulling my leg.

"So he sent you instead?"

"No. I wanted to meet you. We were all sitting at Chipotle and he told everyone that he was going to see you, and then the car came and he bailed out so I knew you would be crushed and I decided to come over and cheer you up." He smiled.

"Maybe you two want something to drink," Carlos said. "A lemonade?"

I definitely wasn't into lemonade." And I was crushed. The boy was right. He wasn't the Knight. Not even close.

He was just an ordinary kid. Short and chubby. And uninvited.

"I know it looks weird. But here I am," he said cheerfully, seeing my bewilderment.

"What kind of a name is Guy?" I demanded from up the stairs.

"Short and masculine, like me," he said.

He was funny. Or at least he thought he was.

"Let's go to the kitchen and have a lemonade," I announced.

I went down and went past him, avoiding his gaze, and he followed me.

I was two years younger than him and he was shorter than me.

What a bummer.

NICE GUY

t was weird. We sat in the kitchen for ten minutes. I didn't know what I wanted to say. And he just sipped his lemonade carefully.

"So?" I said when he was done.

"The lemonade was good," he said. He had big black eyes.

"I know," I said.

"You have a big house."

"It's too big, if you ask me," I said.

"Why?"

"When I was five, a kid got lost here at my birthday party."

"No kidding!" he exclaimed. "How did they find him?"

"They never did," I said with a straight face. "I guess his remains are still somewhere in the house."

His eyes almost popped out. Then he burst with a short nervous laugh. "You're lying," he said. "That's hilarious."

"Not for us. His ghost still shows up for all of my birthdays."

"Yeah, right. I bet it does," he grinned.

"Where do you live?" I asked.

"On Rexford," he said. "A three-bedroom condo."

"What do your parents do?"

"My dad is unemployed. My mom is a nurse at Cedar's."

"Are you rich?"

His cheeks reddened. "No. Pretty average, I guess. My dad says that he saw an ad saying that the City of Beverly Hills is looking for poor people to come live here, because they want to diversify. So we auditioned and they accepted us."

I didn't get it.

"So what happened? They gave you a free condo?"

"Nooo! It's a joke."

"What's diversify?"

"Ask Siri," he shrugged.

"So are you poor?"

"We're okay. We moved here from Covina so my sister and I could go to a better school. It's tight, but we're okay."

"You're the first poor person I've ever met," I said. And then it hit me that Roberta was poor. She was homeless, wasn't she? But I didn't think of her as poor. "But I do know a homeless person."

"We aren't poor. It was a joke." He looked as if he was regretting saying it.

"What was your dad doing before he was unemployed."

"My dad isn't the working type," Guy said. "He is a watcher."

"What's that?"

"He observes life as it goes by." Guy didn't smile, but I had a feeling he was pulling my leg.

"Okay." I wanted to tell him that we were *almost poor* before the show saved us, but he said eagerly, "Can you show me around?"

"Why?" I asked. "Haven't you ever seen a house like this before?"

"I have," his eyes shone. "Almost all my friends live in big homes. But I like to see how people live. You learn a lot and besides, I am the curious type."

"No problem," I said.

We went through the first floor and moved to the second. Five people lived in the house. The three of us and the maids, Gabby and Rosie. The entire staff included Gabby, Rosie, Carlos, Libby, and Marco the gardener. Lately Mom was talking about the possibility of hiring a bodyguard because she was fed up with the paparazzi. She wanted the production to pick up the tab and they refused. She was pissed for a while and swore that they would regret it. I knew she wouldn't give up.

I showed Guy the garage where the new and the old were proudly parked. Boys are impressed with cars—God knows why—and I knew he'd go nuts.

"Eleven cars!" he exclaimed. "Two Ferraris, a mint Jag, two Porsches," he looked like an overwhelmed toddler walking through the aisles of Toys R Us.

I didn't tell him that Dad had to sell his Bugatti to cover some of our debt.

We ended up exhausted in the backyard.

"What's there?" he pointed towards my dad's shack.

"It's my dad's. Where he works." Dad was living there, but I kept it to myself.

"What does he do?"

"He's a writer. He writes for the movies."

"Cool," he said. "Which movies?"

"His last movies were *Zombies Revenge One, Two, and Three,*" I said, waiting to see his reaction. Usually people went out of their mind.

Not Guy. "*ZR One* was cool, but I hated *Two* and *Three. Three* truly sucked," he said. He smiled awkwardly. "Ooops. Sorry."

The door of the shack opened wide and Dad came out. He smiled when he saw me.

"Hi, honey!" he looked at Guy, who looked as if he wanted to vanish into thin air. He looked so miserable I could barely stop myself from laughing.

"Hi, Daddy. This is Guy."

"Hi, Guy. I'm Harold, nice to meet you."

Guy just nodded. "Nice to meet you too, sir," he said in a muffled voice.

"He didn't like your last movie," I said.

Guy looked as if he was going to faint.

"Good for you, Guy," Dad said cheerfully. "I didn't like it either. See you later!"

He smiled, patted Guy's shoulder, kissed my forehead, and went back to his shack.

"I'm sorry," I told poor Guy, but I wasn't. It was actually pretty amusing.

Guy looked as if he had awakened from a bad dream. "He's cool," he said. "But I feel so bad now..."

"Don't," I said. "He's already forgotten the conversation ever happened."

"I'd like to make movies when I'm older," Guy said.

"It's so corny," I said. He knew what I was talking about. Everybody wanted to make movies or be in them. At least in our town.

We crossed the lawn to the gazebo and Guy placed himself comfortably in the hammock.

"I know it sounds corny. But still," Guy said. "I have ideas for movies all the time."

"Like what?"

"Well," he got excited. "I have this movie idea called *The Smart Rebellion*. It's about the day smartphones take control of their owners."

I thought about it for a minute. "Wow!" I said.

"You like it?" he almost fell from the hammock.

"Sounds cool to me," I said. "But what's the story?"

His eyes lit up. "You wanna hear it?"

"Sure," I said.

He told me the story. I hate it when people tell you what happens in a movie they see, but Guy was telling me the story of a movie that hasn't been made yet. And he didn't use the two no-fly-zone magic words over and over again, 'And then.'

He just told me what happened in his movie and it took him twenty minutes.

"It's brilliant," I said when he was done.

He looked like the happiest man on earth.

"You should tell it to my dad," I said. "Let's go."

"Really?"

"Why not? He can give you some advice on how to turn it into a real movie."

He jumped off the hammock and followed me to the shack. I knocked on the door. "Dad, can Guy and I come in?"

"Not now, sweetie!" Dad was saying from behind the closed door. "I'm busy."

I assumed he was drinking.

"Never mind," I told Guy. "You'll tell him next time."

"Okay," he looked a bit disappointed.

It was late, and he needed to get back home. Carlos wasn't around so I used Dad's Uber account to get Guy home. When Dad was drunk and needed a ride he used it and he gave it to me in case he was so drunk he couldn't order himself a ride.

I wanted to ask Guy about Justin the Knight, but there was no more time left. The car showed up and Guy Ubered his way home.

NOW OR NEVER

The three of us were in the media room. Dad watched his beloved Clippers play. Mom leafed through her iPad, and checked her ever-growing social media accounts, and I did my homework quietly, my antennas up in the air. It felt tense, but I loved this rare hour when all of us were together doing our thing and behaving like a real family.

It didn't last long. Mom was trying, again, to push Dad to the limit. She was pitching the idea of marrying him in the show's finale.

"I'm not getting married ever again," Dad said with a sly smile, looking at me and avoiding her gaze.

"You're enjoying this, aren't you?" Mom fumed.

"Being married?" he asked. "It was fun once," he said. "Not anymore."

He still didn't bother to look at her.

So Mom had no choice but to come up with the only logical solution.

"What about divorce?" she asked.

Dad moved his gaze to the game on the screen.

"Who is getting a divorce?" he asked.

"You and me," Mom said triumphantly. "I think you should ask for a divorce so I will get some sympathy from the audience."

"You might get the opposite reaction," he said. His voice didn't show any sign of anxiety. "They might think that the bitch is finally getting what she deserves."

He still didn't look at her.

"Great," she said. "Even better. Anyway, don't you think it's genius?"

"Borderline genius," Dad said, but I don't think he meant it.

Mom wasn't ready to give up. I could see the wheels turning in her head. "Divorce will be huge. America will be hooked on our story. Divorce is so much more entertaining," she mused. "And it can feed the entire second season with great material."

There was silence for a long minute.

"I think you have lost your mind," Dad said finally.

On TV, someone made a shot for three and the fans at the Staples Center went wild.

Mom rose from the sofa. "You think I'm crazy?" she asked in a low voice.

"Yes, I do," Dad said. Now he looked directly at her.

"If it was your idea, you'd say it was nothing short of brilliant," Mom said angrily.

Or did she? She might have pretended to be angry.

Dad didn't answer. He just let out a long sigh and left the media room.

I rose to leave. I wanted to be with him.

"What?" my mom asked me. "What did I do to piss him off so badly?"

"He's upset because he doesn't want to divorce you," I said.

"Don't be silly! It's not a real divorce!" Mom said with a tense smile. "It's a story line. It'll make the show better. And he knows it perfectly well! We'll pretend we are going to divorce, that's all!"

I thought it was another black lie.

As long as there was a good reason, her lies were justified.

But maybe behind the lie was something real, and that was what made Dad so upset.

"So go to his shack and talk to him," I said. "Tell him it's just for the show."

"He doesn't like it when I go there. He needs his space. You'll understand it one day. Plus, he knows how much I love him. He's just in a bad mood."

I wasn't sure about that. And I wasn't sure he cared anymore.

"I will change his mind," Mom said. "You'll see."

I looked at her in disbelief. She looked encouraged.

"He'll divorce me," Mom said. "On the show that is, and he'll thank me later."

Dad didn't want to talk about it, so I asked him if he wanted to go out for a ride. Get some fresh air. He looked surprised.

"Where to?" he asked. It was eight p.m. on a Wednesday. "Shouldn't you go to bed soon?"

"Let's grab something to eat," I said. "And I'm not going to sleep before ten thirty anyway."

"Really?"

He didn't have a clue. I could have told him anything I wanted.

"Okay. Give me ten minutes. I need to change."

He needed a shower badly.

He saw the look in my eyes. "What?" he asked.

"A shower would be a good move," I suggested.

He looked embarrassed. "If you say so," he mumbled.

He was sober, or so I hoped, driving his mint 1989 Jaguar down Beverly Boulevard to his favorite sushi place. Café Sushi wasn't trendy and the food was far from fancy. It had been there forever and Dad had been a regular back in the days when he was a starving screenwriter.

Except he was never starving, as Grandpa Hilton pointed out. Dad left LA to study at NYU's film school and dropped out after two years because, as he told me, "I was eager to start doing the real thing and write for the movies, not just talk about them." Grandpa Hilton was furious about Dad's decision and he cut his allowance until he changed his mind "and got his ass back in school."

So Dad began his starving period, which he claimed lasted a couple of years. Grandpa said it lasted a month because Dad got money from his mom, Grandpa's second wife, Louise, who died when I was a baby.

I was glad that I made him go with me to dinner. We sat at the bar watching the sushi chef prepare our meal and Dad looked happy and told me stories he already told me before, about his starving days.

"You were so happy then," I said.

"Yes, I was," he agreed.

"And why not now?"

I took him by surprise, but my question didn't put him off.

"As I grow older, I find it tougher to be happy," he said after he thought hard about it. "I have less illusions about life. I feel I have less options."

"It's sad, isn't it?"

He didn't answer. Maybe he was regretting telling this to me.

"You are still young," I said. "You have a ton of options."

He smiled a sad smile. It was time to change the subject.

"I want to meet Aunt Roberta again."

He looked at me with a frown. "You like this woman, huh?"

"Yes," I said. "She is the smartest and funniest woman I've ever met."

"Really?" he shrugged. "I have to admit, I don't know her well. Since I started dating your Mom, I saw her maybe twice."

"Let's go look for her," I said.

"When?" He looked puzzled.

"Now," I said. "I know the name of the shelter where she stays downtown."

He was caught off guard.

"And let's bring her dinner."

I looked at him with my pleading look. He drained his sake cup.

"Okay," he said with a determined look. "But if we go to the shelter we should bring lots of food for the other folks as well."

I wanted to kiss him. And I did.

"You are the best," I said.

He ordered a ton of sushi to take out. We waited for another half hour and he told me more stories about the best time of his life.

He winced when he saw the bill and I knew it must have cost a lot. But he didn't say anything, just signed the slip and asked the waiter to help us place the food on the back seat of the Jag.

"Thank you," I said.

"Thank you, my girl," he smiled at me and steered the car toward downtown.

I wanted to scream with excitement. I asked him if I could, because I didn't want to make him lose control of the car and end up in a terrible accident. He smiled and opened the sunroof for me and I stood and screamed my lungs off and, to my surprise, Dad followed me with a long howl. We looked at each other and laughed until tears welled up in my eyes. It felt amazing.

It was a night I will remember for a long time. I'm not saying "as long as I live," because when I go to Grandpa's old folks home I see people who still live but their memory has already died.

Speaking of Grandpa, I forgot to tell my dad his whereabouts and I knew I should, although they hadn't been on speaking terms for ages. Grandpa just sent me a text with a picture of him standing in a field at the edge of what seemed like a jungle, his arm resting on the back of a cow. He had a big grin under his Dodger cap. "Dear Alexa, I'm in heaven," he wrote. "I'm not coming back anytime soon! Stay safe. Love you! Grandpa." The cow looked quite anorexic though.

Later, I was in my bed ready to sleep after a long shower. It was almost midnight and I just wanted to close my eyes and relive every moment of this evening. It wasn't a total failure, although we didn't find Roberta. We'd left mountains of sushi with the shelter's night manager and she thanked us and said that dinner had been served already but that she would see if there were any sushi lovers still awake and ready for a late-night treat. The shelter looked like a school building or a hospital to me. There was nothing even close to what I was expecting, like seeing a ton of miserable people walking around. It was quiet and clean and friendly looking.

I showed the night manager pictures of Roberta on my phone.

"Roberta? Of course I know her. Everyone here does," she said with a wide smile. "She left a few days ago." I told her that Roberta is my aunt and asked if she knew when she'd be back, to which she said, "No, Roberta never tell us her plans, she just comes and goes on the fly, but if you want to get in touch with her, you can call her. I have her phone number somewhere."

I saw Dad's eyebrows arch in astonishment, while the manager looked at her rolodex. He didn't know that Roberta was a self-appointed homeless ranger. I wasn't sure I was free to tell him what Roberta had told me.

"Oh, here it is," the manager said.

I thanked her as if I had just won the lottery and stored Roberta's number in my cellphone.

We went back to the car. Dad looked like he wanted to tell me something, but I spoke first. "I'm glad we did it," I said. "The entire evening was just amazing."

Dad smiled. "The pleasure was mine. I love you, honey," he said.

ACCENT ELIMINATION

Mom was still fighting the producers to get a bodyguard. She said that the hate mail she was getting was frightening.

People loved to hate her.

She had created a monster on TV, and there was no way out because she couldn't give it up. I knew she was really scared because I read some of the hate mail that was posted online and it wasn't funny at all.

There were also death threats.

"Remember what happened to John Lennon," she said to Dad while we were watching a new lousy film on a Friday night in the media room.

"Don't be ridiculous," he looked at her with a mix of disgust and amusement.

"You can mock me as much as you like," she went on, "But when a crazy fan shoots me at close range on Rodeo while I'm shopping at Cartier, what are you going to say?"

"Great for the ratings," he said avoiding her gaze, "Bad for Cartier."

She smiled gloomily. "Very funny. But look at the downside—the show will be cancelled, and there will be no more money to finance the incredible lifestyle we got. Nada."

Mom brought the dough. She was making money. Dad was useless.

"Dad's new movie will be a hit," I said out of nowhere. "He'll earn gazillions."

The two of them looked surprised.

"Harold, did you finally finish your friggin' screenplay?" Mom demanded, offended that she wasn't in the know.

"It's a new screenplay," I interjected. "Can I tell Mom?"

Dad looked at me with a huge question mark in his eyes. *What are you up to?*

"It's based on an idea of a kid I know. His name is Guy. Anyway it's about a smartphone rebellion. You see, everyone has a smartphone. So one day the phones become so smart they conspire to take over their owners."

"Sounds silly to me," Mom dismissed it with a shrug.

"It's a brilliant idea," Dad said and I hoped he wasn't saying it just to tease my mom. "But you should know, honey," he said to me. "There are lots of good ideas that don't make good movies."

"So you didn't write it?" Mom was lost.

"I'm thinking about it," Dad gave me a wink. He loved the little game of humiliating Mom.

"Guy wrote a synopsis and Dad will make it into a great screenplay!" I said.

"That kid needs an agent and a lawyer," Mom quipped.

"Why?" I asked.

"Because your dad sometimes can't help himself," Mom said and looked at Dad with her 'Gotcha' look. It was her turn in the humiliation ping pong.

He rose from his chair. "Damn it, Luella!" he yelled and his face reddened.

"No reason to get excited," Mom said. "Just saying."

"What's going on?" I asked.

"Your dad was sued twice for plagiarism," Mom said in her sub-zero tone.

"What's that?"

"It's borrowing ideas from other people without their permission and pretending they're yours," Mom continued while Dad sank into his chair. "Some people call it theft," she said with a sour smile.

"And what happened?" I asked. I saw Dad's face and I knew he was suffering.

Before she answered he said, "We settled. Not because I stole someone's idea but because I couldn't survive the bad publicity. I wanted to fight it but my agent, the studio, everyone told me to swallow the pill. The movie was more important than me."

"A million point two worth of a pill," Mom said sarcastically. "That's what it cost us and honestly it makes me want to scream when I think about it. Now. All I want is a full-time bodyguard and I wonder why no one cares about my personal safety, especially you," she pointed an accusing finger toward Dad, who looked at her in contempt and retreated to his shack without uttering one more word.

Finally Mom got what she wanted. The producers agreed to pay the full tab and Mom's bodyguard, Mike, burst into our lives.

Carlos told me the rumor was that Mike was once a spy in the Mossad, the Israeli intelligence service, before he came to the City of Angels to fulfill an old dream and become an action movie star. He looked like a wrestler with cropped hair, a baby face, and kind eyes behind his Ray-Bans.

He hovered stealthily around Mom, while she treated him like her butler, which he didn't seem to mind. The problem was that half of the time none of us understood what he was saying.

Mike was advised by his talent agent to take an accent elimination course to get rid of his heavy Israeli accent. His teacher was a Texan so he acquired a Southern accent instead, which sounded like he was dissecting stones in his mouth.

It was laughable and no one understood half of what he was saying. So now he was taking another course to get rid of the Southern accent.

Mom said she didn't care. She liked him. As she said, "He is willing to die for me and he doesn't have to talk. He just has to stop the bullets meant for me."

Plus she loved being the only one who talked all the time.

I tried Roberta at the number I was given by the manager at the shelter, but she didn't pick up and there was no voicemail. I didn't know what to do so I summoned Guy to a meeting. He said that he had a math test and was too busy, so I reluctantly agreed to postpone it until the next day. I told him that Carlos would pick him up after school. He texted me a smiley in return.

Then I bumped into Mike in the kitchen and I had a moment of brilliance because I knew that, as an ex-spy, he should know how to trace people. That's how they do it on TV, right?

I asked him if he had a few minutes for me. "Sure," he said, a bit surprised.

When he said a word or two I could figure out what it was. The problem was when he tried to connect the words to make an intelligent sentence.

I asked him to talk slowly.

"Is it my accent again?" he smiled sadly.

"Sorry, but yes," I said. He looked pissed but kept smiling. "Maybe you can try and speak with your Israeli accent?" I suggested.

"It has been eliminated," he said and waved his iron-pumped arms in frustration. "That's the problem. My old accent was bad, but not as bad as my new one. The good news is I'm working on a newer one."

"Can you reconstruct your old one?" I suggested. "Like Doctor Gold who reconstructs boobs and noses?"

"No... I'm going for a California fusion accent. This time it's an app so it's all between me and my phone. Hopefully I'll sound a lot like you." He smiled and I knew why Mom liked him.

He was good looking.

"I can help you," I said.

"Really?"

"Yeah. Let's start with you saying everything very slowly."

"Ooo-kkkay," he said. He was obviously trained to take orders.

"Great," I said. "There is a rumor that you were a spy or something?"

He laughed. "No, not exactly a spy. Why are you asking?"

"This is totally top secret, so you have to promise me that you won't tell anyone."

He nodded and looked amused. "I promise."

"Say I need to find out where someone lives and the only thing I know is her cellphone number."

"Easy," he said.

"Easy?" I yelled in excitement.

"Yes. Did you misunderstand me?" He said very slowly, "E-A-S-Y."

"No. I got it. I'm just happy."

"Would you like to know how we do it?" He was speaking so slowly that it was starting to get annoying.

"No. Just do it! And you can speak a bit faster," I couldn't help it.

He smiled. "Sorry. Give me the number. I'll get you an answer in half an hour. Good, eh?"

"You are a genius!"

He looked surprised. "Really? It's..." he scratched his head so I chimed in before he could tell me his life story. "You can really get me her address in half an hour?"

He smiled again. "Yeah. I'll make a phone call or two and they'll crack it."
I didn't want to spoil the moment so I didn't ask who *they* were.

As promised, an hour later there was a knock on my door. He knocked three times as spies often do. I opened the door and he gave me a piece of paper.

"Cracked," he said and smiled again.

I looked at the paper and my eyes went wide.

"No, no, it's a mistake," I cried out impatiently.

"Why?"

"It's not the name of the person I'm looking for. It says Darlene Mathews. My aunt's name is Roberta."

He asked me if it was okay to come into the room. I sat on the carpet and he sat on a chair that was a bit too small for him.

"Tell me more," he said.

I felt I could trust him, so I told him everything I knew about Roberta. He was a good listener. He didn't interrupt me for a second.

When I finished he said, "Well, the cellphone number you got at the shelter belongs to Darlene Mathews who lives in Santa Barbara. You can Google map her house. It's near the beach. And I have her picture as well." He punched a couple of keys on his cell phone and showed it to me.

I freaked out.

There she was, looking at me from the screen with a broad smile.

"It's her, eh?" he said triumphantly when he saw the look on my face.

He loved to finish his sentences with this *eh*.

"Aaah," I said.

"Aahh, yes?"

"Aaah!" I whispered.

"Sometimes we get upset when we discover things," he said. "Actually, it happens a lot."

He wasn't just a bodyguard. He was a friggin' shrink!

"It's annoying," I cried out. "She lied to me. I'm about to hate her."

"Wait a minute. Maybe she had good reasons not to tell you everything. From what you've told me, she likes you a lot."

I felt like crying so I thanked him and asked him politely to leave me alone.

As the door closed behind him I said, "Thanks again for your help. You're awesome!"

"No problem," he answered but it sounded more like "No proberm."

Another lie. What color is fitting to illustrate stuff people don't tell you when they tell you the "truth" about themselves?

I Googled Roberta's new name and found out that she was a sculptor and painter. Her one-story Spanish house looked nice from the outside on the Google Street View. I even saw pictures taken at the gala opening of her last exhibition, and then I got to her website.

She had lots of pictures of her art. The first thing that came to mind was garbage. A plastic bag, half empty, overflowing and torn. And a supermarket cart filled with trash. A shabby baby doll looking gloomy. Each painting had a number. When I looked carefully I noticed that it was always the same number: 0812850200.

The more I learned about Roberta's other life, the less angry and the more curious I became. She was a person I looked up to. And she must have had her reasons for being a homeless person in LA and a respected artist in Santa Barbara. She was both— the penniless Roberta from Skid Row and Darlene Mathews who commanded 20,000 dollars for a painting of a plastic bag filled with trash. In my opinion, there was nothing special about her paintings. They looked as if anyone could paint them. Except me. My talent in art isn't something I can brag about.

Anyhow I wanted to see her badly and talk to her. I had to find out why she didn't tell me who she really was, and I wanted to know who the real Roberta was.

I wondered if a person who lives a double life and doesn't tell their close friends about their other life would be considered a liar. The more I thought about it, the more I couldn't make up my mind. It was a question I needed to ask Roberta. She would know the answer. Right?

Next I checked the *Contact* link on her website. And hoped she read her emails.

A GALLANT VISIT
AND ONE MORE

Heavy rain fell all night over our drought-stricken city. "It's about time," gasped the weatherman on TV.

When I woke up and opened the window, the sun was shining again and the day looked bright and crisp, as it always does after a rain.

While I got ready for school, I couldn't stop thinking about Roberta. I knew I had to find a way to meet up with her again.

I thought about it for most of the day and almost forgot I had invited Guy to come over. I texted Carlos to pick him up from school but Carlos called back and told me that he was busy running errands for Mom.

"So what should I do?" I asked him.

"No worries. Call the Beverly Limo Service. We have an account there. Talk to Rhoda. Tell her who you are and what you need." He gave me the phone number and hung up.

Rhoda was nice and said they'd take care of it. She also said that she was a fan of the show and especially Daffodil whom she loves. "You are so smart," she told me, trying to get me to confess to being Daffodil.

"Thank you," I said. "But you didn't hear it from me." She sounded happy when she said, "It's our little secret, right?"

"Yes," I said.

She sent out a stretch limo. Don't ask me why.

But it wasn't Guy who popped out from the back door.

The kid who came out was taller, leaner, and handsome.

He looked up and saw me staring at him from the terrace on the second floor. It was so embarrassing that I wanted to bury myself right there.

He smiled and waved.

I waved back.

Then he made his way to the veranda, which is what Mom calls the front porch, as if he had done it a thousand times before and I couldn't see him anymore.

The knight rode into my house. No horse and no armor though.

I went to the closest mirror and was horrified to see the stupid look on my face.

I had to go down to meet him.

I had no other choice.

I took a big breath and went down to the first floor and into the hallway.

And there he was. Justin the Knight himself.

"Hi," he said.

"Hi," I said.

It felt awkward for a moment.

"Do you want to come up to my room?" I asked.

"Ye-e-es," he said.

He was more nervous than I was.

"Follow me." I said. I climbed the stairs and he followed a step behind me.

"Where is Guy?" I asked.

"I-I," he said. "He-he couldn't co-me."

Oh my god, I thought. He was stuttering so badly I felt sorry for him.

"Don't worry," I said. "It was a bit strange that you bailed out the first time, but it's okay you showed up this time, I guess."

I wished I wouldn't have said the last words.

"It's not something we do all the time," he said and smiled.

We entered my room and sat on the floor.

"It's a mess, sorry," I said. Actually it was pretty tidy, but I needed to break the ice.

He didn't say anything. Just stared at the room avoiding my gaze.

"So what's up?" I asked.

"Nothing much," he said and at least he had stopped stuttering.

"What would you like to talk about?" I asked. He looked at me as if I just landed from Mars.

"Can I w-watch TV?" he asked. His eyes glinted. "The Raiders are pl-pl-playing Colorado?"

Clearly he had a speech impediment of some sort. At times he looked like he was about to choke before he could finish a word.

But he was cute.

"You can do anything you like," I announced. I gave him the TV remote and he quickly found the right channel and looked relieved and happy.

"Are you into it?"

"Into what?"

"Into sports."

"No," he said with a straight face. "My dad makes me play. I hate sports."

I was ready to tell him how much I felt for him, but he snorted a short laugh. "JK. I love sports. Soccer, football, basketball, hockey, baseball. You name it."

"Oh," I said disappointed.

"But I also have a sensitive side," he said softly.

"Like what?"

"I'm allergic to e-e-everything that isn't sport," he was definitely pleased with himself.

"Funny," I said. I still couldn't figure him out.

He was glued to the screen, so I asked him to tell me about the game and he explained every move and every call and when he did, he didn't stutter at all. I noticed that he rarely looked at me and I guessed he was shy or maybe I needed Mom's hairdresser to upgrade my ordinary looks.

I didn't care much about the football game. For me they were a bunch of big guys wearing spandex and helmets, running around and jumping on each other like excited toddlers on a playground.

Sports was as boring to me as knitting.

The game lasted for ages and, at a certain point, I fell asleep.

I woke up and saw him standing by me holding a tray.

"What happened?" I mumbled. The smell was infectious.

"Nothing. You dozed for the rest of the game. I went down and made your favorite drink."

"And what is that?" I rubbed my eyes.

"The c-c-consensus was that it's chocolate milk. So here it is, with a fresh chocolate chip cookie." He placed the tray on the floor besides me.

"Thank you. That's very kind of you," I said.

"I know," he smiled.

I drank the chocolate milk, which was prepared exactly as I liked it.

"Who made it? Gabby or Rosie?"

"I did," he said. "Rosie just showed me around the kitchen. I like to cook. It's fun," he said.

"If you say so." I wondered what was really wrong with him, because as my father told me, every character has a flaw.

"Daffodil," he said out of the blue. "Was it your idea?"

"Yes, why?"

"B-because it's a smart choice for a nickname."

"It's the name of the girl in the show, not mine, hence it's not a nickname," I said.

He grinned. "I guess you don't want to be famous, which for most people in the world would seem strange. B-but I got what you are t-trying to say."

"What?"

"Narcissus, the son of the river God from Greek mythology. He fell in love with the reflection of his face he saw in the river and he literally f-f-ell into the water and drowned," he smiled at me. "And Narcissus the flower is what we call a daffodil."

"Bingo," I said. How could he be good looking and smart and not full of himself? That was a mystery to me.

"I love Greek mythology," he said.

"Daffodil is wearing a mask so she can't see herself," I said quietly.

He looked at me. "You can take off the mask. I don't think you'll fall in love with yourself."

"I'll discuss it with Daffodil. I'm curious to know what she thinks," I said cheerfully.

"I'd love to be on TV," he said, "Playing soccer or football. With my real name all over my jersey."

"Go for it," I said.

"Yeah, I wish." He shrugged. "In my family everyone is into medicine— my Grandpa, my parents. And they talk to me as if it's my destiny too."

"My dad is also into medicine," I said.

"Really? I thought he was a screenwriter."

It was a bad joke. Dad's medicine was in the bottle hid behind the screenplays.

He looked at his phone. "I should get going—it's a bit late. I have to finish a ton of homework."

I was sad but I just smiled so I wouldn't spoil the moment.

I saw him leave and my head was buzzing with thoughts. I was antisocial and I was proud of it. But in a few days I had become friends with two guys. Both of them were nice. I didn't want to think about who I liked more or who I wanted to see again because it gave me a headache. Maybe I'll invite both of them next time and pit one against the other like two gladiators and see what happens.

Just picturing the scene made me chuckle.

And it felt good.

Downstairs, in the kitchen, I bumped into Dad who was sitting by the counter munching on a turkey sandwich.

"Hi, honey."

"Hi, Dad."

He wrinkled his forehead. "I thought about your idea, the smartphone rebellion. I kinda like it."

"It isn't my idea, it's Guy's."

"Who's Guy?"

"You met him, don't you remember?"

"Now I do. It's that friend of yours who should have gotten an agent," he said and looked amused.

"Yeah," I said. "Mom's idea."

Was I imagining it or had his face twitched again?

"Anyway, I'd like to meet him and see what he's got."

He probably had drunk a glass or two, but he looked fine. I knew he was thinking about Guy's idea quite a bit, but he wanted me to think it wasn't that important to him.

"When?"

"Now, tomorrow. Anytime," he shrugged.

He was stuck on his own screenplay, unable to finish it, or even worse, make something good out of it. He needed something to stimulate his artistic juices.

"Maybe he can come over now."

It was still early evening. Why not? I texted Guy to come over.

Guy texted back seconds later. "Why?"

"Nothing. Justin is cool. Thank you."

"Really???" he answered back. "Just kidding."

"My Dad wants to hear your movie idea."

"Wow!"

"Are you coming or not?"

"Now??? Wait, I need to ask my mom."

Sure enough, ten minutes later he was heading to our house. His mom dropped him off and left before I could meet her.

He entered the kitchen with his iPad under his arm and a stupid grin on his face.

"Why are you smiling?" I asked.

"Am I?" he chuckled. "I'm going to pitch my movie to the biggest screenwriter in Hollywood, that's why."

"Stop! Don't be silly," I said. The truth was that Dad was always struggling to write a screenplay that would make money. There was nothing great about that, except the fact that people in this town adored people who knew how to make these kinds of movies, the kind that broke box-office records. They were all artists who bowed down to the dollar. I heard my dad saying it more than once, because he wanted to be free of it, but he couldn't. The studios wanted him to create one moneymaker after the other, and he feared he wasn't able to do it anymore. And it pissed him off that no one cared about his writing. The only thing that mattered was whether his words could turn into gazillions of dollars.

When you see what money does to people, you realize that you should hate it. I know I am too rich to complain, but at the same time I know that everyone here is miserable as hell.

Guy and I walked into my dad's shack.

Dad acted as if he was surprised to see him.

"Oh, it's you! I've heard so much about you," he said with a broad smile, but if there was a fake detector it would probably have exploded at that point.

They shook hands. Guy blushed and looked like a ripe tomato.

"Alexa told me that you came up with a movie idea. Can you tell me about it?"

"Sure," Guy said. "I need a TV to show you my storyboard."

We all went inside the media room, and it took Guy a couple of minutes to set everything up.

What he showed us was a moving storyboard, with Guy's voiceover adding to the pictures with cool music and sound effects.

Ten minutes later, 'The End' appeared. I clapped enthusiastically and Dad joined me.

"Bravo," he said and I knew he meant it.

Guy let out a heavy sigh of relief. "Thank you," he said.

"You did this yourself?" Dad asked.

"Yes, sir."

"All of it?"

"Yes. It's pretty easy," he wasn't boasting, just telling the truth.

"I'm sure it is," Dad said with a chuckle.

He closed his eyes and I knew he was as excited as I was.

"I think that with the right treatment, it can become a great movie, and maybe even a franchise," he said. "And this is the stuff the studios are interested in. Big expansive stories that kids your age must see in theaters, with the most amazing special effects, 3D, and lots of great action."

"But my story ends in one film," Guy said. He looked worried.

"Not necessarily." Dad said. "I can see a franchise here, and with all due respect, this is not a movie yet. It is not even a screenplay, either. You need a skilled writer to turn your idea into a screenplay first."

I wondered if I was witnessing Dad selling himself to a thirteen-year-old kid.

"Mr. Goldsmith, would you do it?" Guy asked eagerly.

"I sure can," Dad examined his fingernails carefully. He needed a manicure in my opinion. "The question is: do I have the time to do it."

I felt pity for poor Dad. I knew he was dying to do it.

"I think Guy needs an agent first," I interjected.

"Really?" Guy said. He was blown away. "Why?"

I had to protect him. I'd explain it to him later.

"Good idea," Dad agreed thoughtfully. "But if Guy is okay with it, I can pitch it to one or two studio heads, just to check if there is any interest. Oftentimes we tend to get overly excited and the decision makers show us the door. So before we commit, let me make a couple of phone calls."

"Whatever you do, Mr. Goldsmith, will be great," Guy said. He was mesmerized by my father's lips, as if God himself was talking to him.

"But you should keep it utterly confidential," Dad said.

"Sure," Guy said.

"You can tell your parents I suppose," I said.

Dad looked at me as if he wasn't convinced.

"What?" I asked.

"Give me a couple of days. Let's keep this between the three of us until I get a solid response," Dad pleaded.

"No problem," Guy said.

I looked at Dad and felt bad. He had lost so much of his self-confidence. I didn't know how Guy would keep it from his parents or his sister or from his best buddies. This was so exciting it could drive anybody crazy.

Dad said he was going to drive Guy home. They could talk more about the movie. He wanted to get a grip on Guy's vision.

Vision? Really? I wanted to tell Dad to give us a break, but I looked at Guy's face and I didn't want to be a party pooper. I made the connection. It was great that Dad was interested. But I wanted it to be right for Guy.

I waved goodbye to them. Dad was the nicest person I knew. It was about time he could become himself again and the hottest writer in town. He deserved it.

A GREEN LIE

For the next episode of *Cruella,* I decided to play a little game. I wrote, on cardboard cue cards, quotes taken from stuff people had posted about Mom.

I explained to Bruce the director what I wanted to do. "What do you think?" I asked.

"I like it a lot," he said with a wry smile. "I mean, it's disgusting, but it's great."

I began at the living room, standing by a huge oil painting of Mom. The camera showed the wide shot, with me looking small and ridiculous in my mask and my jeans and a t-shirt with the caption *'Get a Life!'*

"And action," Bruce said.

"As I told you, dear viewers, you are watching trash," I began. "But you are no longer passive. Thanks to social media, you are creating trash of your own."

"Raise your voice," Bruce said.

"What? I can't hear you," I teased him.

The camera zoomed in as I pointed to the first card.

"This one is very straightforward," I continued. "Cruella, you should die a slow and painful death. Rot in hell!"

I let the card fall and continued, my mask hiding my feelings. "This one was posted by Christine F. So thank you, Christine, for your honesty. In a world of duplicity and dishonesty, you are a breath of fresh air!"

I moved towards the kitchen and the camera followed me. I stopped by the naked armless Aphrodite statue and I showed the next banner.

I read: "I love your show, Cruella, because you are such a cool bitch! I hate to say it, but I won't be surprised if someone shoots you some day. Love KKK."

I moved around the house, making stops and reading more hate posts. Each card I read got nastier and more hateful.

I saw from the looks of the crew around me that they weren't amused. The producers were whispering to each other, probably checking to make sure my stuff wasn't too much for their soapy show.

My last stop was Mom's shrine. An entire wall of her massive bedroom was covered with a ton of pictures, magazine clippings, newspaper reviews, and anything else relating to Mom.

I summed it up, and this time, my voice was trembling a bit. I could feel tears welling in my eyes. "You hateful crazies and psychos out there—you deserve this show and this show deserves you. But remember, it's only a TV show, and behind it are real people who might get hurt. So stay out of our lives, you punks!"

I didn't say I hated them. If you're preaching not to hate, you can't hate, right?

But I did hate them, with all my heart.

Sorry, I'm not the Dalai Lama.

I dropped the last card to the floor.

The film crew clapped and cheered.

"It was great," Bruce told me. He hugged me and said, "You're taking the show to another level."

"It's so low, it's not that big a deal," I shot back at him.

He laughed. "No, I mean you take the entire reality show category to the next level. It's brilliant. You deserve an Emmy."

I shrugged. I wasn't sure he got what I was trying to say. Or maybe he did, but he was obsessed with the ratings and getting awards. You don't become a director without a huge ego. He was doing a trashy show, but still he wanted it to be the best trashy show on TV, so when he's old he could look at his award collection and feel proud.

Was he listening to what I was saying? I was truly afraid that something bad would happen to Mom or to us.

I was terrified of the mean-spirited people waiting out there in the dark, spitting hate. I shivered and ran back to my room and threw the stupid mask on the floor.

I had gotten sucked into the show. I hated it, but I couldn't give it up. I needed to talk to someone sane who would make sense of it. I had to talk to Roberta.

Santa Barbara was just a two-hour drive away. I pictured myself knocking unannounced at Roberta's door and it felt cool.

I had an idea how I'd get there, but what would I do if she wasn't there?

I came up with a plan. I created a phony Gmail account for Ms. Brown and I sent Roberta an email saying that I saw her website and I loved her art. Was it possible to come from LA to her studio to have a closer look at her work?

I signed it Ms. Julie Brown, which was my art teacher's name. I thought it was appropriate to use her name for this very special occasion.

Now both I and Roberta/Darlene were even.

I think that all the lies I came up with would be colored green. They were for a good cause and green was the color of good causes unless you hate Greenpeace, nature, and your neighbor's front lawn.

I was anxious for the next thirty minutes until her reply landed in my inbox.

Dear Ms. Brown, You are welcome to drop by. I'm at my house, which is my studio, most of the time. Just let me know before you leave LA. Thank you for your interest.

Darlene

She added the address and driving directions and that was that.

I read her email many times. It was so cool and so easy. I was excited, but at the same time I felt like throwing up.

I was going to see Roberta soon and I was scared.

My green lies were swelling like hot air balloons. The lies intertwined and became a thick, sophisticated web of deceit. I had to think about all the angles and all the possibilities and I was enjoying it. I was spreading green lies all over the place, and that didn't put any pressure on my conscience or make me feel guilty. Because it was all for a good cause. Right?

GRANDPA STRIKES AGAIN

While in the Philippines, Grandpa threw a bomb at us— so to speak. He got married to a woman there. He instructed his lawyer, Art Hurvitz, to notify the family and requested no one send him presents.

He always had the last laugh.

I didn't think this piece of news would make a big splash in our circles, because no one except me seemed to care about Grandpa.

Boy, I was wrong!

There was an additional piece of news which made everyone nervous. His new bride, twenty-five years of age, was expecting a baby boy, which would be my dad's half-brother and my future uncle.

I thought it was hilarious.

But Grandpa's grown-up kids from previous marriages weren't so amused.

A hasty meeting was held at our home. In attendance were Dad and his half-brothers. I hid behind my old gal, Aphrodite, and listened intently to their heated talk. The three brothers, who were old enough to be grandparents themselves, despised their father.

Grandpa was right. All they cared about was his vast fortune. And now they were worried that they'd never get their hands on it.

I remembered that Grandpa told me that he wouldn't leave his fortune to them. But Dad and his two older brothers, Mark and Don, weren't giving up.

Don was a stockbroker and was doing well, until he got tangled up in a lawsuit for stealing money from his clients. Grandpa said that Mark, his other son, perfected the art of not doing a damn thing his entire life. "And he isn't fun either," he complained.

The three half-brothers sat around the kitchen table with grim faces, sharing a bottle of wine. "There is too much at stake," Don said. "But we have an opportunity here."

I heard them concocting their vicious plot. They would file a complaint with the FBI against Joe, Grandpa's caretaker, for kidnapping his old, senile patient and bringing him to the Philippines in order to take over his assets. They wanted to get Grandpa back, establish that he was unable to take care of himself or make sensible decisions, and get hold of his fortune.

"Hilton should do whatever he wants to do with his money and what is left of his miserable life," Dad tried to say in the beginning of the discussion.

I didn't like what he said about Grandpa, but at least he didn't want to steal from him.

Good for you, Daddy, I thought.

But it only took ten minutes of arm twisting and Dad caved in and joined his brothers' plan.

And I knew why. He was scared that his brothers would get to share the estate and he'd be left out and look like a moron. And this thought was too much for him to bear.

I was so disappointed. Grandpa was right. Dad was a weasel.

There wasn't any love between the three brothers. The only thing that united them was plain old greed. And I was so disgusted I wanted to cry.

When the meeting was over, I sent Grandpa an email, congratulating him for the great news, and adding a few words of warning.

I knew Grandpa was smarter than his kids. But I had to warn him. I just couldn't let them get away with stealing Grandpa's money.

On Saturday around noon, Guy and Justin asked me to join them at the Grove for a movie. They weren't sure what movie. "Come over and we'll see," Guy texted me.

There was nobody at home who could give me a ride so I Ubered down the hill and met the boys at the valet stand. I got out of the car and saw them standing there. When I came closer, they looked as if they were regretting the idea. I don't know why. I swear, they looked really disappointed.

"What?" I said. "Something wrong with the way I look?"

"No...n-n-no!" Justin protested. "You look great!"

"You do!" Guy said and blushed.

I wasn't fishing for compliments so I left it there.

We went to the Apple store and I was bored to death while the boys checked out the new iPhones. Then we strolled into the Farmers Market and ate hot dogs. Pretty soon it became clear that the entire thing was a mistake. Justin and Guy were talking to each other most of the time, goofing around, laughing at each other and everyone around us as if I wasn't there. They didn't even try to impress me.

It was weird.

We couldn't agree on which movie we wanted to see. And by the time we agreed to watch the new *X-Men* movie, it was sold out. I didn't want to stay for the next screening so I said I had to go.

When I watched them from the car, they looked relieved. I wanted to cry.

Guys.

They are so hopeless.

UP NORTH

On a sunny Monday morning, Rhoda from Beverly Limo Service sent over a black sedan driven by a guy named Pat to pick me up. It was President's Day. No school, and I was more than ready to embark on my trip.

Last night I told Mom that I was planning to spend the day off with Jessica, my friend from seventh grade who moved to Calabasas. I told her I had booked a limo to shuttle me to her place and back because her mom couldn't pick me up.

"I might stay for a sleepover," I told her. "I have a late start on Tuesday."

A dish of green lies served to perfection, and that was only the beginning.

Mom was sitting in her bedroom in front of her mirror, getting ready to go out to a movie premiere. Her private makeup artist and hairdresser, Michelle, was making her look gorgeous.

"Who's Jessica? Do I know her?" Mom didn't look at me. There was someone more important in the mirror.

"Why would you?" I asked.

I knew I was right because she didn't care much about my social life. She never made it to any school event or PTA meeting, starting with kindergarten, and I couldn't remember if she had ever set foot inside my school.

Mom had a thick skin. She wasn't offended.

"Is she nice?" she asked as if she read my mind.

"Yes, she is. And her mom is great. And they both love the show."

"Really?" she smiled. Flattery always worked miracles with Mom.

"And I didn't even tell them that they have bad taste," I couldn't help it.

Mom laughed. "You better not, sweetie," she said.

"Is it okay?"

"Yes, it is okay. Should I talk to her mom?" she said.

"If you want to," I said. "She's very nice. But I should warn you. If you call her she'll talk to you for an hour about her days as an aspiring actress. And you'll have to be polite."

"Yeah, I'm not sure that's such a good idea," Mom let out a grumble. "But leave her phone number with Libby in case you need me."

It didn't make much sense, but it was okay with me.

"How do I look?" she asked when Michelle finished her last touches.

"No one would ever guess that you are forty-five," I said.

I couldn't stop myself. She looked at me with her crazy look. "Who says I'm forty-five?" she asked in a harsh voice.

"I just read it this morning on your Wikipedia page," I said.

"What?" she jumped from the chair pushing Michelle aside.

"I'll kill her!" she screamed. "Where is she? Libby!" she yelled. Libby was in charge of Mom's social media stuff.

I disappeared. I needed her to be engaged so I could go on with my plan uninterrupted.

Dad quipped once that Mom had been thirty years old for the last forty-five years.

Poor Libby. I had planted Mom's real age on Wikipedia a day earlier.

When I told Rhoda that I needed a car to drive me to my aunt in Santa Barbara, she asked me kindly if she could call my parents and make sure this was okay.

This is where I knew I had to be clever and lucky. If she spelled out the words Santa Barbara to Mom, my plan would be doomed. I gave her our landline number and asked her to call in five. I waited near the phone with my recording app ready and a knot in my belly.

The phone rang promptly and I picked up. I touched the play button and my mom's voice, which I recorded, said "Hello?" I used her grumpy version.

"Ms. Goldsmith? It's Rhoda from Beverly Limo."

"Make it short, I'm in a hurry," Mom barked. I loved this one. And if you think I had to wait a long time to get it in a dozen different versions, you'd be wrong.

Rhoda made it very short. "I need your approval for Alexa's trip to Santa Barbara."

"No problem," Mom said in her commanding, harsh voice.

And I hung up.

A few seconds later, Rhoda called me back. She sounded shaken.

"I talked to your Mom and she approves."

"I know," I said. "I was there. I'm sorry she was a bit rude. She's always like that before a premiere."

"No problem, hon. Trust me, I am dealing with egomaniacs all day long," Rhoda confided. "And your mom is pure gold in comparison to the others, without naming names."

If she meant it as a compliment it was fine with me.

We settled for the time and place and I let out a huge sigh of relief.

An hour later, I texted Mom from the back seat of the car. I knew that she would never check on how I was doing. I knew I just needed to text her later that I was fine and remind her that I was away because she had already forgotten it the minute I told her.

Pat, the driver, offered me drinks, fruits, and snacks. I thanked him and plugged in my earbuds, and he smiled and didn't bother me. I guess I fell asleep at some point, because I didn't remember much of the trip until he woke me up speaking in a soft voice.

"We're almost there," he said.

"Where?"

"Your aunt's place."

"Really?"

"Yes." He pointed outside. "This is Santa Barbara."

We were driving alongside the ocean.

"It's so beautiful," I said.

"It sure is," he agreed. "I love the ocean. When I was your age I spent most of my time surfing."

"Do you still do it?"

"I wish," he said with a sad smile.

He looked about my father's age and I heard in his voice the same frustration.

I guess every kid dreams of being a grown-up one day and yet it seems that so many grown-ups would love to go back and be kids again. Could it be because they discover that being a grown-up isn't so great? But would they choose to stay kids forever or just start again and do it differently?

It was scary how many unhappy grown-ups there were around me.

We drove for a few more minutes and turned down a small street when I saw the house on the left.

Pat stopped the car. My heart beat fast. I just sat, stuck to my seat, motionless.

"We're here," he said. "This is the house."

"I know," I said.

He looked at me through the rearview mirror and tried to figure out why I wasn't moving.

"I need a couple of minutes," I said.

He nodded.

The house door opened and Roberta came out barefoot wearing a long white dress.

Two dogs came running out as she walked towards the car. Pat jumped out and opened my door.

It was time. I threw on my backpack with a shaking hand and stepped out.

I saw her eyes widen for a split second. The dogs were first to jump on me.

Roberta smiled a big smile, came over, and hugged me.

"What a great surprise," she said. "I missed you so much!"

"Me too," I said with a choked voice. "I came to see your paintings."

She burst out laughing. "Ms. Brown from LA?"

"Yes, sorry," I said and blushed.

She looked at me amused.

"I had to see you," I said sheepishly.

"I'm pleased to see you, Alexa," she said. "And so are Monet and Manet," she pointed to the dogs who were all over me. "You should have said you wanted to come; it would have been okay."

I blushed. "Your phone didn't work."

"It's off most of the time," she said. "Does Jane know?"

"No."

"You're quite an adventurer," she said. I was glad she didn't say I was a schemer and a liar.

Pat was standing there. I hoped he didn't hear the conversation.

Roberta went over to Pat and shook his hand. "Darlene," she said. "Nice to meet you."

She didn't waste time and asked him his plans.

"I need to drive Alexa back," he said. "I'll wait in the car."

"Nonsense. Come in and join us for brunch," she told him.

He shrugged. "I guess that's a yes," Roberta said and Pat smiled.

I felt relieved. Roberta seemed in a good mood.

"Come in, you two," she said. "And please take off your shoes before entering."

DARLENE

Much of the house was an open space almost empty of furniture. One huge painting covered one of the white walls. Just the painting, nothing else.

"Wow!" I said.

"What?" she asked.

"Your house," I said.

"Nothing like yours," she laughed.

We followed her to the backyard. In the very back I saw a mountain of trash. In the front she proudly showed us her organic micro farm.

A huge hen jumped out from behind the bushes. She had a red comb and a suspicious look.

"Marie Antoinette," Roberta announced. "She won't bite you. Don't worry," she muttered when she saw my jaw drop.

"I've never seen a live chicken," I mumbled.

Pat pointed to a goat that was grazing in the very back.

"Oh," Roberta said. "That is Frida, my goat. She's really nice and makes excellent cheese."

She showed us the produce she was growing. Tomatoes, arugula, lettuce, carrots, onions, and herbs. She bent down and named each vegetable as she pulled them gently from the ground.

"Don't my veggies look amazing?" she said with pride.

I nodded. My usual encounters with fruits and vegetables were on the plate. I felt a bit stupid, but it passed quickly. It wasn't my fault, was it?

"They taste even better," she said. "You'll see."

Yeah, right.

Pat helped Roberta in the kitchen, while I arranged the table in the backyard trying my best not to screw things up. Thirty minutes later, we were having a great brunch by a beautiful cypress tree.

It was the best brunch I ever had, with omelets made of Marie Antoinette's eggs and Frida's cheese and an amazing fresh, homemade bread. And Roberta's veggies were really delicious.

The adults talked about their love of the ocean and the sweet time they had growing up in the sixties. It was nice and friendly, but I wanted to have my aunt to myself.

She looked at me and knew exactly what I was thinking.

"Pat, Alexa and I need to be by ourselves for a while. Could you go down to the beach for a couple of hours?" She was direct without being rude and he said "Sure," and jumped to his feet. Roberta patted him on his shoulder. "Good boy," she said and he smirked.

I was finally left with my aunt.

"First you must tell me how you managed to get here," she said.

I told her about my green lies. How I found her and how I schemed my way up to Santa Barbara. She didn't look amused, which made me feel a bit edgy. She listened, her eyes looking at me the entire time. I tried not to avoid her gaze. I feared that she didn't approve of what I did. And I did my best not to tell her half of the truth.

"You are very clever," she said when I finished. "I'm glad to see you, but I'm appalled to hear that you couldn't talk to your mother and tell her the truth."

"You don't understand," I protested. "Mom is too busy to deal with this kind of stuff. All she is concerned with is herself."

Roberta looked disturbed. "I was never a parent myself. But it seems to me that you have to find a way to make your Mom more engaged in your life."

Easy for you to say, I thought. I fought the tears by changing the subject. "Why do you have all this junk here?" I pointed to the piles of trash in the back.

"What people deem worthless is valuable to me. Their garbage is my treasure," Roberta said.

"To me it just seems like junk, and it also smells bad," I said.

"I can't do much about the smell," she said and we walked over to the junk pile. She pulled out a broken rusty kettle and showed it to me. "Look at this kettle. It worked hard for years, helping its owners feel good, brewing their tea and coffee, and one day it broke and they threw it out. For me it's more than just a piece of metal and plastic. It's infused with memories, feelings, history. It has a soul. And one day I might breathe new life into it."

"So you go down to LA and pretend to be homeless just to find treasures that people get rid of? I bet you have a ton of junk here in Santa Barbara."

She stared at me for a moment.

"There is a reason why I do what I do," she said. "You see, there is Roberta, and there is Darlene, and probably a few more in between. But it is my own business. You have things you keep to yourself, and so do I. Everyone has. And our secrets are sacred, a place where we can be true to ourselves, no need to share with others, and no need for colorful lies."

She didn't want to lie to me and she didn't trust me with her secrets, and it hurt.

She asked me to join her inside her studio, which used to be a garage. "This was the reason for your visit right?" she joked.

"Not entirely," I said.

"My art speaks for me," she said.

She showed me her paintings, one by one, and I realized that she was giving me a key to her life. I wasn't sure what to say. I didn't like them very much. I felt awkward and I was thinking of something to tell her that would make her feel good. But coming up with a white lie to a woman like Roberta was hard. I knew she wouldn't buy it.

"I don't get what you do," I said.

"What do you feel when you see the work?" she asked and I knew she was challenging me.

"I feel that I don't like it. I don't even know why," I said.

"You are awesome!" she exclaimed and hugged me. "You know," she said, "by telling me what you really feel you showed me that I'm important to you and this is the best compliment I could have wished for."

She took me by surprise. But I should have known better.

I spent a few more hours with my aunt before I felt it was time to leave. She didn't invite me to stay for the night. At first I was upset, but I realized at some point that it wasn't going to happen. I saw in her eyes that she wanted to be left alone.

And then she just said it: "I think it's time for you to go back home."

She hugged me to soften the blow.

"I am a very private person," she said, trying to explain.

"Who, Darlene or Roberta?" I asked in a muffled voice.

She laughed.

I slept all the way home and no one saw me when I came into the house well after dark. I stayed awake for a while thinking about the trip. My head was swarming with thoughts and images and words and I knew I needed time to figure it all out.

I had taped Roberta when she talked about her art and I took pictures of her paintings. I wanted to print out the pictures and have a closer look.

Someone knocked on my door.

"Who is it?"

"Mom."

She came in looking very glamourous and hugged me. "I missed you so much," she said and sat on the bed. She didn't mention the trip so I guessed she forgot about it.

"Me too. What perfume are you wearing?" The scent was so disgusting I wished I had a gas mask.

"Cruella, Beverly Hills," she said proudly.

She never ceased to amaze me. "Since when?"

"We're testing it," Mom said. "Like it?"

"It's a bit too sweet for me," I said, not wanting to put her off.

"You hate it," she said cheerfully, "But thankfully you are not my demographic."

I definitely wasn't. By demographic, she meant women of all ages with cheap taste who adored her.

"Weren't you supposed to be at a sleepover tonight?" she said offhandedly.

I was stunned.

"Yes," I said. "But I decided to do something much better."

"What?"

"I paid a visit to your sister, Darlene."

THE COLOR OF TRUTH

I swear I didn't plan to tell her the truth. It just leapt from my lips before I even had the chance to think it over.

"What did you say?" Mom was taken aback.

"I went to Santa Barbara to see Aunt Roberta."

Mom's eyes glowed and she hugged me. "That was so nice of you!" she exclaimed. "How is she?"

"She is great," I said, trying to hide my huge surprise.

"I know how much you are fond of her," Mom said. "But truth be told, I wish that someday you will look up to me."

"What do you mean?" I knew perfectly well what she meant.

"You adore her."

I didn't answer. But I knew what was coming.

"I wish we could be closer," Mom said.

I hugged her because she looked so miserable in that brief moment. She was the younger sister who wanted to be loved. She envied her older sister and had unfinished business with Roberta. Any shrink could tell you that.

"I love you, Mom," I whispered in her ear.

"Thank you, honey. I love you too." She looked relieved, but I wondered how I could look up to her when she was so self-obsessed. What valuable lesson would I learn from her, ever?

"Did you know she lives in Santa Barbara and she's an artist?"

Mom wasn't sure. "I might have," she said, "I lost track of her a long time ago. We aren't that close you know."

"Do you want me to tell you about my day with Roberta?" I asked excitedly.

She let out an enormous yawn.

"Sorry, hon, it was a long day. No... not now. I need to go to bed, I have a big day tomorrow." She gave me another air kiss and vanished.

I went over the pictures of Roberta's paintings. Some of them looked identical or almost identical. All of them had the same number: 0812850200. Each painting was of an item, photo-like and realistic. She tended to paint the same subjects. A series of trash bags, a series of broken toys. A red car without wheels. A bunny that was missing its ear. A little drum with a hole in the middle. A supermarket cart with a baby doll sitting in it. The shabby doll looked like a real baby, his face frozen and his eyes wide open and lifeless.

Another series of paintings were close-ups of street signs. She played with the street names. Letters were missing or changed. Wilshire Boulevard was We'll Share Boulevard. Santa Monica became Santa Money CA. Main Street was Mine Street.

There was a story there, hidden beneath the images. But I couldn't quite figure them out. Then I remembered the first time I saw Roberta pushing the cart up the hill and I realized it must have had something to do with her walking the streets and seeing things.

I knew that artists did some crazy stuff to get inspired. Maybe living a homeless life inspired Roberta's art. But why was she coming down to LA? She could have been inspired in Santa Barbara. Was there something special in Los Angeles that attracted her?

I had to go back to the shelter, have a word with the people there. The manager had said that everyone knew her. Someone down there might be able to explain.

It took me a while to fall asleep. Mom's reaction to my confession made my entire scheme look foolish. I could have asked her to go visit Roberta to begin with.

Anyhow, after telling so many colorful lies, it was refreshing to tell the truth for a change.

But what is the color of truth? It turns out, I knew it all along.

Truth has no color. It's transparent.

And with that lighter-than-air thought floating in my mind, I fell asleep.

The next morning when I got ready for school, it hit me. No more colorful lies for me. Just the plain, simple truth.

I promised myself I'd try it, for at least one day.

As usual, Libby was on the speaker with Lizzy while I was supposedly not paying attention.

"My boss is into something big," Libby said victoriously to her fiancée. "Last night he sold a huge project."

"Which project? To whom?" Lizzy's voice went a notch higher.

"*The Smart Rebellion*. I can't disclose the name of the studio, but it's the one on Pico."

"Fox! For how much?" Lizzy snorted.

"Low eight. Based on a two-page pitch."

"That's huge! What's the premise?"

"Smartphones go to war on humans."

"Brilliant," Lizzy said enthusiastically. "When can I go out with it?"

"Later today when I know more! Love ya!" said the traitor who took me to school.

She sent her a couple of voice kisses and the one that came back sounded like a fart.

I sat frozen in my seat. My heart racing, I checked frantically to see if I had gotten any texts from Guy in the last twenty-four hours.

There were none.

I texted him, asking if my Dad talked to him since our last meeting.

"Why? No," he answered back.

"Just checking."

Libby dropped me off at school. I knew I had to act fast.

"Have a great day," she said cheerfully.

I pulled up my hoody and gave her my most nasty look but she was already off. I went to a corner to avoid the stream of students who were pouring into school.

"Dad, I need to talk to you," I texted frantically.

No response.

"Dad, it's urgent!"

Nothing.

I was desperate, but I had to go to class.

It took Dad an hour to respond. I was making my way to history class when I got his text.

"What???"

I called, standing in the corridor trying to filter the background noise with the phone tucked into my ear.

"You signed a deal on Guy's project?"

He was thinking for a few seconds.

"No, not yet."

"Are you sure?"

"Who told you?"

"I have my sources," I said.

He laughed. Apparently, he was in a good mood. "I reached an understanding," he said reluctantly. "But it's verbal. Nothing set in stone."

"What about Guy?" I hated when he danced around.

"What about him?"

"Did you secure him in the deal?"

He didn't answer.

"Did you, Dad?" I tried not to lose my temper.

He still didn't answer.

"I hate you!" I yelled at him and got a few bewildered looks from students who were strolling up and down the corridor.

"Hey! No need to be so angry, hon. We'll talk about it when you're back home," he said.

"I recommend you fix it," I said, "Because it's going to appear in *The Hollywood Reporter* later today."

"No way!" he said firmly.

"Yes way. Ask your loyal assistant. Her fiancée works there, as you probably know!" and I hung up.

At noon, while I was munching on an apple in the cafeteria, I was able to text Guy and set up an urgent meeting with him at three o'clock at Chipotle on Beverly Drive.

Before school got out, I managed to talk to Cruella's publicist, Jeanine. I told her I had a great story and asked her to get in touch with *Variety* or

Deadline. I demanded she not disclose her source and swore her to secrecy. I knew she would do anything to please me. I told her what I had and she wrote it down. I needed my story to appear before Lizzy's.

She hesitated. "Do I need to talk to your dad?" she asked carefully.

"No," I said. "He's cool. I brought the two of them together," I bragged.

She was thinking. "Look," I said, "If you don't want to do it, just give me the contacts and I'll do it myself."

"I'll do it," she finally said.

She called me back and told me that my story would go out everywhere in the next twenty minutes.

"You are a doll," I told her. "Love you!"

I wondered if I should tell Guy exactly what was going on, and then I remembered that I had decided to tell the truth and it felt good. Truth could be cruel and hurtful but I had to give it a shot, before I went back to my beautiful rainbow of colorful lies.

I had a feeling Guy would be capable of handling the truth.

THE PAINS OF TRUTH

We sat across from each other at Chipotle. Guy nervously glanced around at the other tables, filled with noisy boys.

"What's the matter?" I asked. "Sitting with me won't wreck your reputation."

He just reddened. What else is new?

"Let's get down to business," I said. "My dad isn't playing it fair, so we need to strike first and make it hard on him to claim that he came up with your brilliant idea."

He looked confused. "What happened?"

"Nothing yet, but just in case. And by the way, you need an agent."

He nodded. "Yeah, I talked to my dad and he promised to get in touch with a guy he knows from college."

"Too late. You need an agent yesterday."

He smiled. "And I'm guessing you already sorted it out."

"I did something without asking you," I admitted. "Because every minute counts. The news will hit the trade's websites very soon."

"What's that?"

"Hollywood's media. It'll say, a movie pitch by Guy Green, a thirteen-year-old kid from Beverly Hills, and Harold Goldsmith, the A-list Hollywood screenwriter, ignited a bidding war among the big studios. It will mention that you don't have an agent yet."

He looked stunned.

"In a few minutes, every agent in town is going to be looking for you," I said. "You'll hire a top agent and he'll sort out the best deal for you."

"Did you come up with this yourself?" he looked at me with well-deserved awe.

"Why? Do you want to compliment me?" I asked. "Just say it. I love compliments."

"How did you do it?"

"I listen to so much of this crap in my house, I know a thing or two about this town. But I can't invent a story like you did. That is beyond me," I said.

"I want to be a director when I grow up," Guy said sheepishly. "That's all."

"I think you just made a huge step forward in that direction," I said.

He smiled. Sometimes people don't know how good they are and they need someone else to tell them. It's so simple, really, but for whatever reason, people find it difficult to do.

"How do I know which agent to pick?" he asked.

"Choose the biggest A-hole with the most famous clients. You can't go wrong with that."

He listened intently. Then his phone rang.

He looked at the screen. "It's CAA."

"Agents!" I cried out. "Pick it up!"

"Hello," I heard him say. "Yes, this is Guy Green." He listened. "Hold on," he said, and shoved the phone under his butt and sat on it.

"What do think you're doing?" I burst laughing. "Are you going to hatch mini iPhones? Answer the damn call!"

"So they wouldn't be able to listen," he whispered. "They want to meet later this afternoon. They'll send a car to pick me up."

"Do it. But don't say yes right away. Take meetings with all of them before you commit, and take your dad with you."

"Okay." He picked up the phone, "Hi, sorry, I need to talk to my parents." He listened a few more seconds and said, "Thank you, I'll call you right back." He hung up.

"What did he say?"

"The guy said not to talk to anyone else before they meet me."

"And what did you say?"

"Just thank you. Actually he seemed nice."

"No way, you got it all wrong," I said. "They can't be nice."

Jeanine sent me a couple of links and I forwarded them to Guy. "You are already famous," I said. "Look at your phone." He looked at the first story and his eyes widened. "Wow," he said.

And his phone rang again and again. And again.

I found Dad in the kitchen nursing a drink, although it was hardly three in the afternoon.

"How was school?" he asked in a cheerful voice. I knew he was putting on an act. I threw my backpack on the floor. "You hate me, don't you?" I said.

"No! Why?"

"Daddy!" I raised my voice in frustration. I wanted him to tell me the truth. No more BS to hide his real feelings.

"Okay... okay. I was mad as hell half an hour ago when I saw the news you planted."

I wasn't going to apologize, because I was damn proud of myself.

He continued, "I told Libby to find out who did it, otherwise she was toast, which she is anyway. So she found out." He let out a few expletives to describe how he felt about Libby and sipped some more from his glass.

I filled a glass with water and ice and sat opposite him. "I had to do it," I said.

"Actually, I am quite proud of you," he said and I believed him.

"Why didn't you tell the studio about Guy?"

"I couldn't," he said. I could tell he was embarrassed, but my frankness made it easier for him to tell the truth. "It was too hard to tell them that the first great concept I came up with in three years wasn't mine. That it was written by a thirteen-year-old kid and I'm just feeding off his talent. It's pretty humiliating, don't you think?" he took a sip from his drink.

I knew how he felt but I couldn't find any sympathy for him.

"No," I said. "Just sign the deal, get it done and you'll be on top again. Guy will follow your lead. And you can do what you are good at. Writing."

He wasn't convinced.

"He's getting an agent as we speak," I said. "The worst thing that can happen to you is to have his agent tell him to do it with someone else."

He looked worried. The thought had crossed his mind already.

"I won't let that happen," I said, "But you need to come to your senses."

"How *old* are you?" Dad asked with a sad smile. "Almost twelve."

"Are you sure?"

"You should probably know, unless I'm not really your daughter."

He hugged me and laughed.

A couple of days later it was all sorted out. Dad was quite surprised to find out that his collaboration with Guy didn't take anything away from him. On the contrary. It brought the project a lot of publicity and gave Dad the exposure he had longed for all these dry years. And he didn't complain about the fat check he was given. He was a provider again. It was no longer just Mom who made piles of money.

And Guy became the top money-making student in the Beverly Hills school system. Not by being the son of a rich person, but because of his talent and hard work. And if *The Smart Rebellion* ever became a hit, he would wind up a very rich dude. That's what his A-hole agent told him.

When Guy told me what happened, I couldn't have been more proud. I made my dad and Guy happy, and it felt amazing. And I knew that the movie would be huge. But it wasn't just about the money. Both of them loved what they did. And Dad was climbing back from a dark pit. Life had started to make sense to him again.

There was only one person who didn't cope well with the situation.

Mom was not happy.

"Now that you are once again a big-shot screenwriter," she said bitterly when the three of us were at Angelini's for a Friday night dinner, "I guess my chances of getting you on board the finale are not looking good." It was weird to see her so jealous.

"I'm not going to remarry you or divorce you in front of the entire country, if that's what you mean," Dad said. He looked self-assured and I wanted to applaud in support.

"You don't give a damn about my show," she fumed. (This is, of course, the edited version of what she really said.)

He remained unfazed. "I do. I'm happy with your success, Luella, but I won't do it and you'll have to respect that."

"I need a phenomenal last episode. If you're such a great screenwriter, why don't you give us a brilliant idea? Do it and I'll let go of my worthless ideas. Or maybe you need a thirteen-year-old kid to help you?"

Now he lost it.

"Shut up," he said, his fist clenched. "I'm fed up with your bitching and moaning."

People from other tables were turning their heads.

"Okay," my mom said. "I've had enough. I'm leaving. Alexa, are you coming with me or staying?"

"I'm hungry," I protested. "I want my pasta first."

"Okay. You stay with your father," she snorted and left in a hurry, almost crashing into a waiter who carried a tray full of dishes.

Dad shrugged. "I'm sorry," he said.

"No worries, Dad. She'll get over it," I said.

"Maybe. But I'm afraid I won't," he said. I looked at him and it was clear to me that he was super angry this time. He actually might make the move and leave Mom.

But I didn't feel bad about it. As a matter of fact, I didn't feel anything at all.

The waiter placed the amazing "Nonna Elvira's" lasagna in front of me.

Call me selfish, but I am familiar with my family dramas, and if I have to choose between this heavenly lasagna and my parents' relationship, I'll go with the lasagna.

BREAKUP AND HEARTBREAK

Things went downhill from there. Dad moved out to a seaside hotel in Malibu. He told us he needed time and space to work on the screenplay. Mom was acting weird. She was sick for a few days, staying in bed and telling everyone that she had the flu while making everyone around her really sick.

Libby, who wasn't fired after all for leaking discrete information to the press, was now the go-between for my parents. She continued to discuss everything in the car with Lizzy, oblivious to my presence. Maybe she didn't realize I was telling on her to my dad, or maybe, even worse, my dad just couldn't confront her.

Libby told Lizzy that my mom suffered a mental breakdown and it was my dad's fault. Lizzy told her that it was a show. "Just wait and see. She'll make a huge story out of it," she said. "This woman needs attention."

Lizzy was spot on. When I saw the first tweet, a shudder went through my spine. I ran upstairs to Mom's bedroom. She was sitting in bed wrapped in her silk gown, working on her multiple smartphones. She didn't look sick at all. She looked quite happy and pretty.

"Did you see it?" I said breathless.

"What?"

"TMZ tweeted that Dad left you and that you are suffering from a nervous breakdown!"

"No need to worry," she almost yawned. "It's all speculation and gossip. Bad people."

"Who is responsible for this?"

"Who else?" Mom said casually. "I leaked it."

I looked at her, stunned. She didn't even lift her eyes from her cellphones to look at me.

"Why?"

"You need to feed the beast, honey. I have a show to promote."

"So you aren't sick? It's all fake?" I fumed.

She made a face as if what I said had a sour taste. "I am sick. I am hurt. I suffer. And the fans have all the right in the world to know how I feel and show me their sympathy."

"And what about Dad?" I demanded. "He didn't leave you. He's just taking time to write the screenplay."

She shrugged. "I'm sorry, honey. Dad isn't coming back anytime soon."

"What?" I screamed. "Why didn't anybody tell me?"

"Ask Dad," Mom said. "It was his decision."

Something didn't ring true.

"Dad should know that I'm hurt. He behaved like a spoiled child," Mom continued, seeing me agonizing over this as she was trying to explain.

"You want him back?"

"Of course I want him back. But make no mistake, he wants me even more. When he comes to his senses, he'll crawl back." She believed every word she said.

I sat at the edge of the bed trying to make sense of what she just told me.

"So nothing is true. It's all a show," I said.

"I love your father," Mom said. "That's what matters."

"He didn't leave you!"

I heard a ding. She looked at her gold-plated phone.

"Now he did," she said and when I looked at her eyes I saw she was scared.

I ran out to my room and called Dad.

"What's going on?" I yelled. "You just told Mom you're leaving her?"

He was trying to control his anger.

"I just confirmed what she already told America."

"So you are getting a divorce?"

"I just wanted to be left alone for a while and your mom is making things harder for me."

"Where are you, Dad?"

"I'm down in San Diego. I need a day or two to think things over. The media is chasing me. I can't write. I can't think. It's crazy," his voice trembled.

"I'm sorry," I told him.

"Don't be," he said. "It's not your fault."

He told me how much he loved me and I succeeded in holding back my tears until he hung up.

The story of my parents' divorce propelled in the media like a tornado. I was so devastated I didn't want to see anyone and it was easy because no one wanted to see me either. I was trying hard not to pity myself and I succeeded for about a second during each passing hour.

Late at night, I was scrolling through Instagram when I saw something that made my blood freeze.

Justin with a girl, his arm around her waist and a caption, "Together finally!"

She was pretty and looked older than me.

I looked at the picture in disbelief and started to cry. My tears rolled down my face mixed with a low uncontrollable wail that sounded as if it was coming from someone else's throat. I was shook up and hurt. I was crushed. I was angry. I didn't know what to do. I had never felt like that before. It took me a while until I fell asleep, but it was the first thing that came to my mind when I opened my eyes.

I felt so bad, I wanted to throw up. Outside my window, the world looked beautiful. An amazing winter day in LA. But I was hurting like I'd never hurt before, ever. I needed to talk to someone, but I couldn't think of anyone.

I was wandering around school like a zombie, but I guess no one noticed because I never attracted much attention. I felt a hole in my stomach and each time I picked up my cellphone I was horrified that I might see something that would make me feel worse.

But why? I wasn't in love with Justin the Knight. I didn't know what love was, unless love felt like the hole in my belly. In the movies people look pleased or miserable because of love, but by watching the movies you couldn't tell what love really was. The more I thought about it I realized I was upset because it came as a surprise. If Justin was my true friend why didn't he tell me about his girlfriend?

So I couldn't resist sending him a text, which I regretted the minute it was flying over to his device. "Congrats on your new girlfriend!"

"What?"

"The one on your Instagram. She looks cute."

"Are u crazy? She's my cousin Alma. NOT my girlfriend. She just got off the plane from DC."

I felt so stupid. "She's still cute."

"You want to meet her?"

"Okay."

"I'll tell her. Can I come over tonight?"

"Sure."

"See ya!"

The dark hole in my belly disappeared at once. But there was another feeling. Disappointment mixed with relief.

I waited for school to end and when Carlos picked me up I told him we were going to Diddy Riese in Westwood for ice cream sandwiches and a cookie. I needed something sweet to stay sane.

A SURPRISE VISIT

On my way home, Justin texted that he forgot he had an assignment he needed to turn in tomorrow. "Can't make it," he wrote.

I was upset until the phone rang and I heard the low baritone voice that always made me so happy.

"Is this my beautiful little girl?"

"Grandpa! Where are you?" I yelled.

"Here in LA. Just landed a couple of hours ago."

"Wow! That's awesome!"

"Come see me. We're at the Four Seasons on Wilshire."

"We?"

"My wife Rose and myself. I'm dying to see you."

"Ten minutes," I said and gave Carlos the new destination.

"Hilton is back?" he asked.

"Yes, he is, and we are going to see him."

"I like Hilton," Carlos said. "He's a good man."

I smiled. Carlos was probably the only person in LA besides me who thought Grandpa was a good man.

They were waiting in the lobby. I ran into Grandpa's open arms and hugged him so tight I felt like crying.

Rose looked shy, but she was really pretty. We hugged like old friends. She looked very young and it was a bit embarrassing, but Grandpa looked happy and tanned.

We walked a couple of blocks down to Spago for a bite. Grandpa said that Rose was hungry all the time because of the baby. "She eats for two," he said and she reddened. I looked at her belly and didn't see a bump.

"People say that I look much younger than my age," Grandpa said when we were seated.

"You do look great," I said.

"Well, I tell them I'm eighty-five to make it easy for them to give me the compliment," he chuckled.

"How old *are* you, Grandpa?" I asked.

"Seventy-two," he said.

"You look a bit older," I said.

He laughed. "Really?"

"I hate lies. White lies, red lies, green lies. I want to be true to myself and others. Especially people I love," I said.

"I love you too, honey, but lying to other people doesn't mean that you're not true to yourself. Anyway, I'm seventyfive." He laughed again.

"Are you sure?" I said.

He enjoyed it. "No," he said. "I might be a bit older."

After he finished ordering the entire menu for Rose, he said, "I didn't plan to come back this early, it's all your fault. I always knew I could count on you."

"How's life down there?" I didn't want him to moan about his kids.

"Oh, wonderful! It's so much fun in the village. All of a sudden my life has meaning. I'm useful again. I was elected mayor of the village and I have a lot on my plate. You'd be surprised that we don't have power lines out there. We still use generators. Thank god, they have a cellphone network. Anyway, I'm going to bring the village into the twenty-first century. I have to take care of two hundred people, not including my own herd."

"Sounds impressive," I said. "Seems so much more fun than being in an old folks' home."

"No doubt. Much more fun! By the way, remind me later to show you pictures of my beautiful cows." He looked thrilled. Much happier than the last time I saw him.

"Okay," I said. "I will."

"Anyway," he went back to the topic I was dreading, and his voice turned harder. "I came back because you alerted me that my boys are planning to steal all I got. Tomorrow morning I'm meeting with my lawyers in front of a judge. We are bringing two of the best geriatric specialists in America and a couple of top-notch shrinks. They are going to testify that I'm one hundred percent mentally fit," he pointed to his head. "I'm not a senile old man as these morons claim." He smiled coldly, "I'm going to sign my new will in front of the judge, end of story."

I looked at his wife. She was eating slowly and when Grandpa punched his fist on the table she patted his hand with a calming smile.

"Don't be so angry, Grandpa. It's just money," I said.

He looked at me speechless and burst out laughing so hard he started to cough.

"A lot of money," he said. "My reward for more than fifty years of hard work."

"Yes, but even without the money you are still a great person," I said.

"Thank you for the compliment, sweetie, but you need to be a bit more grounded."

"What does that mean?" I asked.

"Money is important. Money gives you the freedom to do a lot of things in life," Grandpa said. "Especially if you're smart."

"Interesting," I said. "Roberta told me the exact opposite. She said that money is a burden, and the more you have the less free you are."

"Who told you this rubbish?" he snorted.

"Aunt Roberta, Mom's sister."

He shrugged. "Yeah, I know Darlene. I once made a pass at her."

"Grandpa!"

"She was an attractive woman, but a whacko, nonetheless."

"She looks sane to me," I protested.

"Is she still wandering around town disguised as a homeless person, looking for her lost son?" Grandpa asked.

I didn't answer. I just looked at him dumbfounded. What was he talking about?

"Is she?" he kept asking.

"Yes, she's wandering around town. What about her son?" I threw it back at him, recovering from the shock.

"Why should I know?" Grandpa shrugged.

"You seem to know everything," I looked at him intently while he was trying to figure out why it was so important to me.

"Well, she had an unwanted pregnancy when she was very young and after she gave birth, she immediately gave the baby up for adoption. Years later she felt remorse. She decided to go and look for the boy. And she found him. He was a drug addict, homeless, here on Skid Row. He didn't care much about her. He didn't want her help or have anything to do with her. So she started to come down here and lived like a homeless person just to be close to him. And then one day he disappeared into thin air.

I felt the blood in my body freezing. "What happened to him?"

"She came to me one day very emotional and asked me to help her look for him. I liked her, so I tried to help out, but it didn't last long because my people couldn't find him."

"Which people?"

"People I know who can find a needle in a haystack. But they hit a wall."

"So why does she keep coming back?" I cried out.

He shrugged, "You need to ask her."

I was so excited that I forgot all about Grandpa's surprise visit. I wanted to get home as fast as I could and think about what he'd just told me.

"Why are you so interested in her?" he asked.

"I like her a lot," I said.

"She is a bit off," Grandpa Hilton said. "Much nicer than your mom, forgive me for saying, but I wouldn't want you to be influenced by her. She's a free spirit, but you should always keep your two feet on the ground."

"Last I checked, my feet were on the ground," I said. "And what's wrong with being a free spirit?"

Grandpa arched his eyebrows. "In a couple of days, we'll have a conversation. You'll understand," he said, a bit impatient.

Before we separated he hugged me and whispered in my ear, "Everything I told you about the will should be kept in total secrecy. Not a word to anyone!"

"You can count on me, Grandpa," I said.

He flashed a big smile and said, "I know."

A BLUE LIE

I tried to figure out what 0812850200, the number that appeared on all of Roberta's paintings, meant. Thinking about what Grandpa told me, I thought I understood what she was trying to say in them. The supermarket cart with the broken toys. The torn plastic bag. The street signs. The baby doll. It was all about her homeless son. But what was the meaning of the number?

I thought about the baby she gave up for adoption, and years later how she looked for him, found him, but he didn't want anything to do with her. It felt so sad and miserable. I could picture her longing for him during endless nights and how devastated she must have been to be turned down by her own son. And then I thought about him. A woman bursting into his life claiming she was the mother he never knew because she gave him up for adoption.

Not a good start for a friendly conversation.

I looked at the printouts of her paintings and my thoughts drifted to this kid, my cousin. All I wanted to know was what happened to him. Where was he right now? And I had a question for Roberta too. Why did you do it?

We were days from shooting the last episode of *Cruella*. There were endless meetings at home with the producers and the writers and I could hear Mom screaming and yelling and swearing. They were all incompetents, idiots, and blood-suckers. They couldn't come up with any good ideas and she had to do everything herself.

The atmosphere at home was so tense, I was relieved to be at school for half the day.

I think Mom was panicking because Dad wasn't showing any interest in coming back home any time soon. She had announced that they were separating to get public attention and then she realized it was really happening. I think when it hit her she took it really hard. It wasn't a game. It wasn't a show. This was her life. And she was responsible for the mess.

Dad called me up and told me that he had moved into a condo on the Wilshire corridor.

"So you aren't coming home?"

"I need more time," he said. I heard the hesitation in his voice.

"For the screenplay?"

"Yes. But I need to think things over."

"Did you talk to Mom?"

"I sure did. How is she?"

"Crazier," I said and he sighed.

"I miss you." I had hoped he would feel guilty and come back home.

"I miss you, too. See you soon," he said and hung up.

I went into my room and started looking once more for clues to Roberta's missing son.

I was obsessed and I knew I needed someone to help me out.

But who?

Mom texted, "Please come down to the living room. We need you!"

From the look on everyone's face, I knew they had hit the wall.

Mom hugged me. It was a bit embarrassing in front of everyone, but I played along.

"Why do you people look so miserable?" I asked when I could breathe again. I saw the two writers, Josh and Rick; Bruce, the director; and the two producers whose names I still couldn't remember. They all looked as if they wanted to kill themselves with an option to come back to life and start from scratch.

"It's the season finale and we don't have anything worthwhile to shoot," the male producer said in anguish.

Yeah, I thought. There won't be any wedding in front of the cameras. Or a divorce. What a disaster.

"We came up with an idea," Mom said, turning to me, "To expose the real you in the show."

"What? Why?" I tried to keep my cool.

"America, the fans, the media, they all want to know who the girl behind the Catwoman mask is," said the other female producer with a sweet smile. Too sweet if you ask me.

"No. Never!" I said forcefully.

"But it will help the show," Mom said, although she didn't look convinced, "And anyway there are rumors that Daffodil is my daughter. It's your time to be in the spotlight. Enjoy it."

"No," I said. "I regret I did it in the first place. And by the way," I looked at the producers straight in the eyes, "I didn't get a penny from you. So you don't own me."

"Okay, okay," Mom commanded. "Please, everyone, can you all just leave us alone. I need a few moments with my daughter."

"Don't go anywhere," I said. "I have a better idea."

They froze on their tracks.

"If you want America to talk about the finale," I said, "You need something bigger, crazier, and wilder than exposing the girl behind the Catwoman mask."

Mom looked at me intently. "What are you thinking of?" she asked, intrigued.

"Something terrible has to happen to Cruella," I said. They looked at me as if I was out of my mind.

Mom was fast. "Do I need to die?" she asked wryly.

"No!" I protested. "But you could disappear. It can be an amazing cliffhanger for the new season."

"What a sick idea," said one of the writers. I think he meant it as a compliment.

"Brilliant," said Mom excitedly. "I could be kidnapped..." She didn't finish her thought.

"It will backfire," the male producer said. "It's a stunt that will kill your credibility."

Mom was thinking hard.

"Okay," she said. "Let's all go our separate ways and think it over. I think we are on to something huge. And Dane and Gretchen," she turned to the producers. "Alexa is right. You should pay her. Up until now you took her for granted, but as a star of the show she needs to get paid."

Dane and Gretchen?

"But you are getting paid for her," Dane protested. "It's in the contract.

Mom put on a "What the..." face.

"It's Stu, the idiot. I'll kill him!" she yelled.

Stu was Mom's loyal agent.

She was lying, pretending she didn't know about it, and I felt my anger boiling and I instantly came up with a color.

Blue for a lie that makes the people you lie to angry as hell.

I felt betrayed. I thought that Mom's idea to get kidnapped wasn't that bad after all.

And as this thought crossed my mind, she hugged me and kissed me on my forehead.

TOO MUCH TO HANDLE

Grandpa's move shattered our family like an earthquake. Dad called me up and told me that Grandpa had asked his sons to meet him at his lawyer's office. "You have to be there too," he said.

"Why?" I asked.

"I'm not quite sure," he said.

I knew it was going to be fun watching Grandpa rip his naughty kids apart, plus I didn't mind skipping school.

I said, "Okay." I felt bad for hiding what I knew, but I also was glad to be with Dad for a couple of hours. I missed him terribly.

He came to pick me up and the first few minutes were pure joy. He looked sober and clean. He had gotten a new haircut and I told him he looked great and he smiled and nodded as if he knew why. But when we got closer to Century City, I started to feel bad again because I knew he was tense although he tried to mask it with small talk.

"Did you already know that Grandpa was in town?" he asked when we entered the elevator in the glass and steel tower.

"Yes," I said.

"You saw him?"

"Yes."

"How is he?" he asked nervously.

"Looked pretty normal to me," I said, but Dad wasn't paying attention. At the end of the long corridor he pushed open a big wooden door and we were ushered into the conference room of the Arthur Hurwitz Law partnership, where you can enjoy a panoramic view of the City of Angels. It was a beautiful sunny day and the Hollywood sign glittered in the distance.

Grim-looking Don and Mark, Dad's brothers, were already seated. They were a bit surprised to see me.

"No school today?" Don asked me, faking a smile.

"Is it your turn to babysit, Harold? She should wait outside," Mark said with a harsher tone.

Dad looked confused, but then Grandpa walked in with his lawyers in tow and said, "She stays!"

Grandpa sat down opposite his boys. They all looked away as if his gaze was too much for them to handle.

"I suppose I should say it's good to see you, but I don't want to lie," Grandpa said to his three sons. "I have to admit that the three of you have aged significantly since the last time I saw you. Don, you look like you're my age. Mark, your plastic surgeon needs to go to jail for malpractice. And Harold, my dear, drinking doesn't do your liver any good or help the color of your skin."

They looked at him as if he was a ghost.

Grandpa's lawyer, Art Hurvitz, was assisted by two younger guns who ran the show. They all looked sleek as if they had just walked out of an episode of *The Good Fight*, and everyone was smiling sweetly at me. Probably because they had never seen a girl my age in their conference room.

Art's assistant served drinks. I went for tap water with ice, and the meeting started.

I think the stress in the room got to me. I sat on the edge of my seat.

First, each of us got a file with a ton of papers in it. I got one too, with my name on it.

What was going on?

"Good morning, everyone," Art said, "We are here at the behest of your father, and your grandfather," he looked at me and smiled. "Hilton Goldsmith, my old friend and client, who honors us with his presence," Grandpa winked at me.

I winked back.

Art's voice was reassuring and every word was pronounced perfectly. No need for accent elimination here. "Hilton just got married to a very lovely lady and decided to reside with her and their future baby in the Philippines. He also decided to make some changes concerning his estate. We finalized and approved the changes in front of a judge yesterday. In addition, we added affidavits from experts regarding Hilton's mental health, which confirm that he is capable of making these decisions."

Grandpa interfered, "I'm as bright as a lamp and my mind is as sharp as a razor," he made a pause and ended triumphantly. "And it's official!"

The brothers exchanged frantic looks. Grandpa smirked like a kid who had just been given a cone filled with chocolate ice cream.

"To sum it up," the lawyer continued, "Your father and your grandfather," he looked at me again, "Decided that he wants to give away his wealth now, rather than later or after he passes away. Please take a moment and read the documents that are in the file in front of you, unless you want me to read them to you."

"Do I need to read it?" I asked.

"You don't have to do it now," Art Hurwitz said and Grandpa winked again.

"We'll read it ourselves, thank you," Don said with a grave voice.

My dad was pale but he didn't say anything.

They all looked as if a huge dark cloud hung over their heads as they read the entire thing in total silence.

Five minutes later they were all done. And they were staring at me.

Something looked very wrong.

Dad put his hand on mine.

"What?" I asked. "Why are you staring at me?"

"Because," Grandpa said to me with a smile. "These boys aren't getting a penny. Alexa, you are the main beneficiary of my estate. Eighty percent goes to you."

"Over my dead body!" Mark yelled. His face reddened and he jerked his head upward. I was afraid he was going to explode right in front of us.

"That's ridiculous! We'll fight it in court!" Don slammed his fist down on the desk and immediately cried out in pain. The desk didn't even rattle.

Dad just looked white as a sheet. His brothers glared at him accusingly.

"What? I had nothing to do with this," he yelled "I swear!"

"It's all me," Grandpa said, amused. "Harold didn't know a thing."

"It's you!" Don pointed a finger at me.

"Sure it's me," I said. "And this is you, or maybe it's not you?" I pointed a finger at him.

One of the younger lawyers tried to control a laugh and started to cough.

"This girl made him do it," Mark barked, then turned to Dad. "And you knew it all along Harold. You're an accomplice in this travesty!"

"Don't yell at my daughter," Dad said with his best menacing tone. He couldn't compete with the rest, but he tried. "If you're accusing me, you're out of your mind!"

"Stop right there!" Grandpa raised his voice. "Leave the girl alone. It was my decision and I didn't consult with anyone nor was I manipulated by anyone."

"I bet the girl told him that we planned on challenging his sanity," Mark said bitterly. "I saw her hanging around when we had our meeting." The son who Grandpa said wasn't the sharpest pencil in the family couldn't control himself.

"Shut up!" Don screamed at him.

"Your despicable plan didn't work and so you end up with nothing," Grandpa smiled calmly. "You can go now."

"You started a huge war, old man!" Don yelled at Grandpa. "You don't understand what just happened! Let's go, Mark. We have nothing more to do here. You bastard, you'll hear from our lawyers soon. Very soon."

They grabbed the files hastily and left the room.

"I hope it's the last I see of you!" Grandpa called after them.

I felt ashamed. He was their father after all.

"Congratulations, Alexa," said Art Hurvitz with a big smile.

"When all is said and done, eighty percent of your grandfather's wealth, which is roughly estimated today at 200 million dollars, will be yours."

Everyone looked at me with a knowing look. My father was still in a state of shock.

"Do I have to accept it?" I said. "I told Grandpa I don't care about money."

The men in the room didn't seem to take what I said seriously.

"You might change your mind when you turn twenty-one. Till then, just take it as it is," the lawyer said with a smile reserved for pets and babies.

"No reason to decide now," Dad said in a soft voice.

"Thank you, Grandpa," I said and looked into his eyes.

"Come give me a big hug," Grandpa said cheerfully. "I love you so much."

I asked Dad how he felt when we entered the car.

"Relieved," he said. "I don't want to fight with Hilton, and I'm glad that you got it."

I believed him.

"Why don't you and Grandpa get along?"

"He wasn't there for me, ever," Dad said. "And that goes for Don and Mark, too. We have a lot of unfinished business with Hilton. And you are old enough to understand that some scars never heal."

I knew he spoke the truth. His truth. "It's sad," I said.

"This is why I want to be the best father I can be," he said in a shaky voice.

"You are my best father," I said.

He nodded, but he had that tormented look I had seen so many times before.

"I'd like to show you my condo. You are gonna like it."

"Sure, let's go."

A few minutes later we left the car with the valet and rode the elevator to Dad's new place. We were hungry and Dad cooked grilled cheese sandwiches, which were delicious.

The condo was nicely decorated with expensive views of the west side.

"You like it?" he asked.

"Yes. Do you?"

He nodded.

"When are you coming back home?" I asked. He didn't answer.

"Are you divorcing Mom?" There was a lump in my throat.

He didn't answer.

"Are you?"

"I'm still thinking about it," Dad admitted. He hated confrontations. I was afraid he had already made up his mind.

"I stopped drinking," he said.

"Wow!" I said. "Good for you!"

"It's hard."

I didn't want to talk about it. It felt weird. "How's the writing going?"

"Good," he said. "Great, actually."

Later when he drove me home, he told me about the screenplay for *The Smart Rebellion,* but all I could think about was their looming divorce. I knew my dad wasn't happy and I wondered what Mom's reaction would be. I knew she loved him and it would break her heart. And I was also thinking about life without him at home, and it felt horrible.

It was hard because Dad actually looked happier.

I didn't know much about love myself. And I remembered having heard somewhere that love is only one aspect of a good marriage, and definitely not enough for two adults to stay together.

Wait a minute! That was Mom who said those words. On her show. She knew what needed to be done on her reality show, but couldn't do it for real.

What a bummer.

I wanted my parents to live together with me. I knew I was egotistical but I couldn't help it.

For the rest of the day, all I thought about was how I could save my parents' marriage. I couldn't care less about the two hundred million that had just been handed to me by Grandpa a few hours ago.

BETTER OR WORSE

Two days later, someone came from the principal's office and exchanged whispers with my English teacher.

"Alexa, you need to go to the office with Ms. Garret," the teacher said. They both looked grim.

"Why? What happened?" I asked Ms. Garret while we were walking fast through the corridors.

"Your mom's assistant is here to excuse you," she said avoiding my inquisitive gaze. When we entered the office, Libby jumped up and hugged me. I was really surprised to be smashed into her bosom and I've seen enough movies and TV in my short life to know that something terrible must have happened.

"Who died?" I asked her.

"Nobody yet," she said and looked like she wanted to slap herself in the face.

"Grandpa?"

"No, Ian. He isn't dead. He's just sick," she said and looked away.

On the way to Cedars-Sinai she told me that a friend of Ian's found him on the floor of his place and couldn't wake him up.

"You mean he's in a coma?" I cried out.

She didn't answer.

I started to cry.

When we arrived at the intensive care ward, I saw Mom, Dad, and Melissa, Ian's Mom, Dad's ex-wife.

"Where is he? How is he?" I rushed into my dad's open arms. "The doctors say he's going to be okay," Dad said with a quiver, his face ashen. "Can I see him?"

"Later, the doctors are in there right now." Mom came close and hugged us both. For a split second, we were a family again. She pointed to a closed door.

It was then that I noticed that *Cruella's* crew was swarming around, filming.

"Why are they here?" I yelled.

"They're just doing their job," Mom said in her most soothing voice. "They're with us, for better or for worse." The makeup on her face couldn't hide that she wasn't at all upset. She had seen an opportunity.

She didn't have to be kidnapped any more. Something bigger had just happened.

I made my way to Ian's room and pushed open the door. The camera crew chased me but I slammed the door in their faces.

A bunch of doctors and nurses were around the bed. They looked at me in surprise.

"You can't be in here!" a nurse rushed towards me.

"He's my brother!" I cried out.

"Sorry, dear," she said quietly, "You have to stay outside."

"I want to see him!"

One of the doctors said, "Let her." The nurse looked displeased when I reached the bed.

My brother was lying there with a respiratory mask on his face and an IV and a bunch of other cords stuck to his arms. His face was as white as the sheets and his eyes were shut. I knew he was alive because I heard the beeps and saw the line on the monitor working up and down.

I touched his hand. It was cold.

"Ian, it's Alexa," I whispered in his ear. "Wake up, please."

He didn't respond. I wiped my tears with my hand. I felt helpless and desperate. I couldn't do anything. All I could do was look at him and fight back the fear that was building up inside of me.

"He is in good hands," the doctor said and looked into my eyes as if to convince me. "Now you should leave."

"Thank you," I said and left the room with a heavy heart. I was scared.

The bright glow of the follow spot held by the gaffer blinded me. The camera pinned me in its gaze.

I heard Mom's voice say, "Cry, Alexa. Let your feelings out." I looked at the camera and opened my eyes as wide as I could.

"I hate you," I said and blocked the lens with my backpack.

Carlos and Mike were instructed by Mom to take care of me and get me safely back home. I was too upset to protest. Everybody else stayed at the hospital. When I rushed into my room, Mike stood at the doorway with a serious look.

"I'm not going to kill myself, if that's what you're worrying about," I informed him.

"Before you do, let me know. I don't want to lose my job," he said. He definitely had a weird sense of humor.

I nodded.

"I'll be downstairs," he said. "Let me know if you need me."

"Thank you."

The news was all over the internet. They said that Ian had suffered a drug overdose. They said he was a known addict. They also said that his situation was serious and an undisclosed source in the hospital said that his chances of recovery were slim.

I cried for hours. Rosie brought me food and drinks but I couldn't touch them. Empty and exhausted, I fell asleep.

I awoke from a bad dream, soaked in sweat, and let out a cry.

I heard a knock on the door. "It's me, Mike. I'm here if you need me."

"I'm fine. What time is it?"

"Seven thirty in the evening."

It all started to flood in again.

"Can I come in?" he asked behind the door.

I let him in. He was standing there with a miserable look on his face.

"How's Ian?"

"Stable," he said.

"You think he's going to die?" I looked at his eyes hoping he would lie to me.

He didn't answer. I guess he couldn't lie to me.

His eyes fell on the pictures of Roberta's paintings that were spread on the floor.

"What's diz?" he asked.

"What do you think diz is?" I mocked his ridiculous accent.

He looked at the pictures carefully. "Pictures of paintings."

"Bravo," I said. "Very insightful."

He didn't care about me being ironic, or maybe he didn't get it. "It's strange," he said after inspecting each picture carefully. "The person who painted it is homeless. You can tell from the street signs that this is where he used to hang out. And instead of signing with his name on the paintings, he is signing with a date. Am I right or what?"

I jumped off my bed. 0812850200. A date?

"August twelfth, nineteen eighty-five, 2 a.m.?" I shrieked.

"Exactly," he said calmly.

"What does this date mean?" I asked.

He looked again at the paintings. "Looking at ze broken baby toys, it might have somezing to do with a baby."

Bingo. I knew it. "A date of birth?"

"Possibly," he said.

I hugged him. "You are a genius."

He smiled. "I know," he said. "And modest too."

I started to dance around the room. Believe me, I'm not much of a dancer, and Mike kept looking at me funny. Maybe he thought I was out of my mind.

I knew I could trust him.

"Can I tell you what I know about it?"

His eyes lit up. "Please do."

He sat on the edge of my bed and listened. Again, he didn't interrupt me, not even once.

"Incredible," he said when I was done. "And very sad."

"Roberta's son," I asked. "My cousin. How can I find him?"

"He can be traced," Mike hesitated. "Unless he's dead. But that is simple to establish. If he's alive we can track him down, but why? Your Grandpa already told you that he didn't want anything to do with your aunt—his mother. Why should he connect with you?"

"Can you find him for me please, please, please?" I asked and before he could react I said, "Of course you can."

The compliment softened him. "I can try," he shrugged. "And if I do find him, then what?"

"We'll see," I said.

His phone rang. He looked at the screen.

"Your mom is on her way back home," he said.

"And Ian? What about him?"

"The same," he said. "No change yet. Sorry."

HANGING THERE

ruella aired an 'Ian' special the next evening and the ratings shot into the stratosphere. Mom was the happiest woman alive, although she managed to put on a sad face. Lizzy told Libby that seventy-five percent of *Cruella's* viewers didn't think she was a wicked woman after all. In Libby's view, it wasn't great. "She should stay nasty, otherwise why bother to watch *Cruella?*" she wondered.

Poor Ian wanted so much to be part of the show and he got what he wished for, but not on his terms.

But not *everything* was perfect. Melissa, Ian's mother, didn't allow the crew into Ian's room and Dad agreed.

Mom was furious.

"I hate this woman," Mom spat. "This bitter old hag will never forgive me for stealing your father from her."

"Did you?"

"I came to his rescue. Trust me," Mom snorted.

Yet, a picture of my brother's face lying in his hospital bed surfaced on the web. Mom was showing the picture and saying how heartless and cowardly it was whoever did it, and I knew it was her. Her fingerprints were all over that picture if you ask me.

Mom was still pleading with me to appear on the show as myself, but I refused. In the last couple of days, she was busy editing the show while Dad and I were at the hospital, and after the show aired she was too exhausted to spend time at the hospital. She rested on her laurels, which in her case was her imperial bed.

Guy and Justin came to visit at the hospital. They had this somber, awkward look. We hugged and I felt good about my friends. Dad hugged his writing partner and shook hands with Justin.

"I'm so happy you came," I told them. "It's so boring and stressful here."

I told them I was hungry, so we walked over a few blocks to Joan's On Third to grab something to eat.

"How's Ian?" Justin said.

"He's in a coma, but they say he'll come out of it."

"When?" Guy asked.

"No one knows," I said, fighting tears.

"I'd like to be there when he opens his eyes," Justin said. "It'll be so weird because he won't understand why he's there and he'll freak out."

"He'll see you and go back into his coma," I said with a smirk and they laughed. Sorry, I couldn't help it.

"It's like a movie, but it's not," Guy said. "It's real, and it's scary."

We were sitting on the sidewalk and it was good to be among friends. I had a cupcake and the guys devoured a tuna melt.

"I-I w-w-wonder why most of the movies have a happy ending," Justin said, "While in real life things don't end so happily."

"Unless you believe that there is life after death," Guy said.

"But if e-e-everyone is going to die one day, then there are z-z-zero happy endings in l-l-life."

"That's why we need the movies," Guy said. "To forget about what you just said. To give us some hope."

"So a happy ending is a sort of a lie, isn't it?" I asked, while trying to find a matching color in my mind.

They all nodded in agreement.

Orange could fit, because sunset is at the end of the day, yet it is beautiful and magical.

"I finished the tuna melt and it looks like a happy ending to me," Guy said and we all laughed.

A week passed and there was no improvement in Ian's condition. I went to the hospital each day after school, joining Dad and Melissa who were sitting by Ian's bed. Dad was writing his screenplay on his laptop. I admired his ability to concentrate, but he told me that it kept him sane.

I love my dad.

A couple of hours later, I saw my mom from my bedroom window. She stormed into the house, Carlos and Mike in tow, carrying a ton of shopping bags.

It was one of those days when mom's credit cards "needed a bit of fresh air," so she took them for a stroll down Rodeo Drive.

When we were in a dire financial situation and Dad told Mom that she'd better stop her shopping madness, Mom would chuckle and say that the cards took charge of her. But Dad wasn't amused.

Now she had the money and she was free to roam.

"What's up?" I texted Mike. "Any news?"

Minutes later he showed up in my room with a mug of fresh coffee in his hand.

"You look tired," I said.

"It was a long day," he sighed. "All the tourists on Rodeo wanted a selfie with your mom. She has fans all over the world. It's crazy."

"You should enter the stores from the back," I said.

He shrugged. "She likes to mingle with the fans." I knew it made his job so much tougher, but he stopped short of complaining.

"She's great," he said.

"She sure is," I agreed.

White lies.

"Anyway, I found our guy," he said.

I jumped off my bed. "What?! You met him?"

"No," he smiled. "I know who he is and where he lives."

"Wow," I exulted. "That was fast!"

"Yeah. Actually it wasn't that hard. You see, first I searched the internet. There is a ton of information if you know where to look, and having his exact time of birth didn't hurt. I also paid a visit to the shelter and talked to people on Skid Row."

"You hacked into his personal files?" I asked, lowering my voice.

His voice went also lower. "Hacking is a harsh word. I browsed here and there. Mostly there."

I whispered, "Where?"

"There," he whispered back.

"Why are we whispering?" I asked. "No one is listening."

"You never know," he said and looked around.

"You are an ex-spy. No need to hide it."

"If I confess, I would have to kill you," he looked at me with his poker face.

"Forget about it!" I yelled. I knew he meant it.

"Thank you for not putting me in an impossible position," he said.

He punched a key on his phone and showed me a picture of a young man who, no doubt, had Roberta's eyes and chin.

"Here is our target," he said. "Joseph Gaddel. Born August twelve, nineteen eighty-five at two a.m. in Seattle, Washington, to Darlene Walker. Name of father unknown. Was given up for adoption three weeks later and was adopted and raised in Seattle by Judith and Rob Gaddel. Rob died two years ago of a heart attack. Judith, a retired teacher, still lives in Seattle in the house where Joe grew up."

I could hardly control my excitement. "Where is he now?"

Mike smiled. "In Haiti. With an aid organization."

"Why was he homeless?" I asked.

"He started a tech company and put all his money into it, but unfortunately it went down the tubes, and he lost everything. Alcohol, drugs and living on the street followed. He was out and about for a year but recovered and started over again. Seems like a good guy who hit a rough patch and found his way out."

"I bet he is," I said. "I'd like to meet him. I have so many questions to ask him."

"I can give you some useful information," Mike said. "Let's start with his email address."

"You are a genius," I announced.

"I know," he said.

"And very modest," we said in unison.

I was ready and eager to hear the entire story of Joseph Gaddel.

"By the way, your accent has gotten much better," I complimented him.

"I sink you got uzed to it," he said, "but senks anyway."

THE HEIRESS

Mom's mood, which was soaring for twenty-four hours, crashed and burned the next day.

She was at my door before I woke up. Something was wrong, I thought, because it was too early for her to show up.

"Why didn't you tell me?" she demanded furiously. I rubbed my eyes, still under the warm covers.

"What?"

"About Hilton."

"Oh, I thought you knew he was here," I said. Why would she care suddenly about Grandpa? She never asked me anything about him.

She calmed down.

"You don't know what he's done?"

I pushed away the duvet and sat up in bed.

"Yeah, he got married and he's having a baby. So what?"

"No, no," she let out a short raspy laugh. "I'm talking about the big news. He made you his sole heiress. The news just broke out. Your uncles are suing him."

I shrugged. "Oh, he wants to give me a lot of money, but I didn't agree to it yet."

She looked at me in astonishment, her eyes widened.

"What? What did you just say?"

"Can we talk about it later? I'm going to be late for school," I jumped out of bed.

"Sure we can. But first we have to find a way to evade the paparazzi blockade outside."

"Good morning mom," I said and yawned.

She loosened up a bit. "Good morning, honey. I'll wait for you downstairs."

I took a shower, got dressed, and called Grandpa. He told me that they were leaving in a day or two and he wanted to see me.

"Sure," I said. "I'll come over after school. Mom told me that you're in trouble for giving me your money."

He laughed. "Trouble? No. I can handle that. Don't worry."

"You are awesome and I really thank you for the gift, but I'm not sure I can accept it." I said.

"You can," he said firmly. "And you will."

"We need to talk," I said.

"Okay," he said reluctantly. "But you know when I make up my mind it's a done deal."

"I know," I said. "But you told me that there's always room to negotiate a better deal."

He chuckled. "So you want to negotiate? What about?"

"I need to look into your eyes when we talk," I said, "And now I'm late for school."

"Well, now you've put me under a lot of pressure," he said, "When I look into your eyes, I melt."

"You are so sweet, Grandpa. Don't worry, you told me that you always have the upper hand."

His chuckle turned into a roaring laugh.

"I can't wait to see you," he said.

Mom told Libby that she would drive me to school. "We need some mother and daughter quality time," she told Libby. "But I need you as a decoy." She handed Libby the keys to the Tesla. "You drive first," she said. "Gabby will sit in the back seat, and the paparazzi will go after you, thinking it's Alexa. We'll go in your car a few minutes later."

Mom's plan worked perfectly. Libby and Gabby drove out of the gates through a throng of paparazzi and then sped down the hill out of sight, and the entire media army joined in the chase. Five minutes later, the coast was clear and Mom and I rolled down the hill calmly in Libby's Fiat 500.

Mom was overjoyed. "See how I beat them? They are so annoying!"

"I thought you liked them," I said.

"I just use them," she said under her breath.

She spoke the truth, I guess.

"I'm sorry I was a bit off earlier," she said. "I got paranoid hearing the news, and I felt I was left out."

I didn't say anything. She was right, so why interfere?

"Anyway, as your mother, I feel relieved. I know that your future is secure. So whatever your dad or I do, or fail to do, with our lives, you're guaranteed a comfortable future. You know what I mean?"

I knew what she meant.

"Hilton is smart," Mom went on. "You are the perfect heiress to his fortune."

"I don't want to be an heiress. I hate the sound of it," I protested.

She glanced at me, raising her eyebrows.

"There is nothing wrong with being rich," she said.

"I'd like to succeed on my own," I said.

She shrugged and I yawned.

"You didn't sleep well last night, did you?" she asked.

"I had terrible dreams," I lied.

"Really?"

"Yes," the words were flooding out. "I dreamed I was standing in our backyard and heavy rain mixed with hail was pouring down. The hail was made of gold coins. Huge gold coins with Grandpa's face on one side and a smiling cat on the other. The coins hit me hard and I tried to escape but I couldn't move. I was horrified, scared to death, it was awful. And the coins kept falling until they covered me and I couldn't breathe anymore. I cried for help but no one heard me. You were asleep. I guess you couldn't hear me screaming."

"OMG," Mom said. "What a nightmare!"

"Yeah, I know," I continued, "I was all by myself in the dream and I remember thinking that since I didn't finish my homework and I wasn't ready for my math quiz, that I could die peacefully because my grades were ruined anyway. I looked up and couldn't see the sky anymore and I knew it was my last breath and I was about to die, and at that point I woke up and started to cry.

"My baby!" Mom looked horrified, "It's horrible!"

"Yeah," I said, enjoying her panic. "I was shaking in bed like forever. It was sooo scary."

She couldn't find the words to console me. She just shook her head.

"Why didn't you come to me?" she asked. "I'm always there for you!"

"I've never come to you," I said. "Even when I was three years old you didn't like me crawling into your bed in the middle of the night."

"Nonsense," she said. "I freaked out after you came in unannounced one night when your dad and I were making out."

"Yeah. I remember. It was gross," I said and it crossed my mind that now the risk of finding Mom and Dad in bed making out was very slim.

"You might need help," Mom said in her Dr. Phil mode.

"Please don't offer me a shrink," I warned her. She gave me a disturbed look that pleased me. "Next time you have a nightmare, come into my room and tell me everything. I'm your mom after all. Just text me first. "

When school was over, the paparazzi still hung around the school gates like hungry vultures. I put my hoodie up and no one paid attention when I mingled into the stream of students leaving. I met Carlos a couple of blocks down the street and we drove away in silence to the Four Seasons.

We sat in Grandpa's suite. Rose watched a rerun of *Cruella* on TV and when she saw me she giggled. It was so awkward to see the girl with the Catwoman mask on the screen and know it was me.

"I hate that girl," I told her. "She is so pretentious."

She giggled again and pointed her finger at me. "It's you, and you're cute!"

"Thank you," I said.

"What's up?" Grandpa asked.

"I'm being chased by paparazzi," I said, "Because of what you did."

Grandpa wasn't impressed. "It'll go away sooner than you think."

"Grandpa, I love you," I said. "And I don't want you to think that I'm an ungrateful brat. But I am not sure it was such a good idea giving me most of your money."

"It was a great idea," he said. "Trust me."

"I have to tell you something about myself," I said. "You might find it strange, but I don't want to be rich."

"You don't, huh?" he smiled. "That's because you are a normal, down-to-earth girl. Now you don't care about it, but when you get older, you'll change your mind."

"You once said that you wanted to give your estate to charity."

"I did," he said with a growl. "But I had to do something before my sons put their hands on my money, and I had to act fast. And guess what? When you turn twenty-one you can give it away to charity. It's your money. But I don't think you'll do it. You'll get older and wiser."

"Okay," I said carefully, "I get it. How about I give the money to charity now?"

I saw his face darken and I knew what he would say, so I continued, "Not all of it right away. Like, I give twenty million each year until I'm twenty-one"

"So when you are twenty-one, nothing will be left," his growl grew.

"Yes," I said.

He laughed. "I can't accept that," he said. "It doesn't make sense."

"Well, then, sadly I am going to have to pass on your generous offer," I said.

"You can't, it's not in your power to decline," he looked irritated.

"I know that giving me the money now wasn't your only concern," I said.

He sighed. "It's smarter to do it now instead of you having to pay a huge amount of taxes after I die," he said. "But I really want you to have it. I really do."

"I know." It was time to negotiate. "Let's spend eighty percent on charity in the next ten years, and the rest will wait for me to decide when I'm twenty-one."

"Twenty percent to charity and the rest when you are twenty-one," he said

"Thirty-seventy," I said.

He shook his head.

"You are so stubborn," I cried out.

"I'll go to thirty-five, sixty-five. That's my final offer," he said.

"I pass," I said and rose from the chair.

He smiled. "You are my granddaughter all right," he couldn't hide his pride. "You are tough as nails!"

"Thank you. But what about you?"

"Sixty-forty," he said and stretched his hand for a handshake.

"Fifty-fifty," I let his hand dangle in midair.

"We have a deal," he said. We shook hands.

I felt great. I knew that he would agree. Grandpa Hilton was, after all, a reasonable man.

He grabbed his cellphone. "Okay, I'll call Hurwitz and instruct him to make the changes."

"Nice doing business with you, Grandpa."

"The pleasure was all mine," Grandpa Hilton said.

We hugged.

JOE

sent an email to Joseph Gaddel, but for ten long days I didn't get a response. Each day that passed without an answer made me moody and restless.

Carlos and I were headed for the hospital when I heard the swish and saw the new email in my inbox.

"Something happened?" he asked noticing my excitement.

"Wait, what did I do?" I pulled out the earbuds.

"You yelled 'OMG!'" he said smiling.

"Oh, I got an important email," I said. "Sorry."

"Dear Ms. Goldsmith," the email read. *"Thank you for your kind email. I'm sorry it took me so long to respond. Unfortunately, there is no internet connection where I live. I'm now in the capital, Port-au-Prince, running some errands so I am able to communicate.*

I'm very thrilled to hear that you have a keen interest in what we do here. And it's great that you are interested in helping our organization with a generous donation. I'm not sure how and why you wrote me. I assume that you might have bumped into my blog? Anyway, you reached the wrong person. With regard to donations you should contact Ms. Kyla Roberts at our New York office. She is cc'd on this email and I'm sure she'll respond soon.

Thank you for reaching out! Sincerely, Joe Gaddel."

What a bummer. Now I had to deal with someone else. My heart sank. I should have been wiser on how these things work in the real world.

In my email I didn't reveal anything about my interest in him. I didn't tell him that I was eleven years old. For all intents and purposes, I was a woman from Beverly Hills who wished to make a seven-figure donation to the Save Haiti Now Foundation.

Obviously, I didn't think beyond that. But at least he replied. Now I needed to come up with a plan to make him my friend. After all the trouble I had gone through to find him, I at least had to meet the guy.

Mom hired a couple of private nurses to watch over Ian twenty-four/seven, because she argued that Dad and Melissa should get some time off. This was so nice and unexpected of her that no one objected. I thought it was very considerate of Mom, because being at the hospital was taking its toll on Dad and his ex-wife.

When I dropped by the hospital, the nurse told me that everything was normal. I sat by Ian's bedside and looked at his pale face. He was in his own world and seemed very peaceful and I wondered what it was like being in a coma. Was it like dreaming? Or was it like dying with a chance of parole?

I started writing a journal, trying to fill in the gaps. I was planning on handing it to him when he woke up so he'd be up to speed with what he missed during his comatose period. I wasn't sure if he would be interested in what I wrote. He was my brother, but I realized I didn't know much about what he liked or disliked except for being high and listening to music. I'd known him since the day I was born, but what did I really know about him?

Not much.

I made a note in my journal to ask him to tell me more about himself.

I wondered if people around me had lost hope in his recovery. I had no doubt that he would wake up. He was too young to stay in a coma forever.

I wondered if, when he came back, he would change his life. Like go to college or get a decent job. Dying was high on everybody's list as a life-changing experience. Just living was boring, but almost dying was exciting. Coming back from a coma should be an eye-opener. That's why they call it lifechanging. But Ian was too lazy to change his life. Plus, there was no reward attached. He needed something that would be more rewarding than the money Dad was funneling each month into his bank account.

Dad came by an hour later and looked exhausted. He hugged me and told me to go home. "It's late," he said.

I stayed with him for a while. I told him funny stuff and tried to cheer him up. But he wasn't really listening. His mind was somewhere else. I texted Carlos to pick me up.

"How's Ian?" Carlos asked when I got into the car.

"The same," I said. "He is there but he isn't."

"He's a good kid," he sighed.

"He'll be fine," I said.

"God willing," Carlos said. "I pray for his recovery every day."

"You believe in God?"

He looked at me surprised. "Of course I do. You should pray too," he said. "God listens."

His conviction made me say, "I will," and I decided to come up with a prayer before I went to sleep.

Normally, I would have asked Carlos how he knew that there is a God and many more related questions like why God didn't take care of Ian in the first place, but now I thought it was pointless and disrespectful.

Back at home, I returned to Joe's email to try to figure out my next step. I thought about the many colorful lies that were part of my life. My mind drifted to the obvious solution, a big lie. A master lie. Call it the rainbow lie made up of all the colorful lies. I wanted badly to meet Joe and to make him a friend of mine. I wanted him to meet Roberta. I wanted to correct what was broken so many years ago. This was a story where I wanted a happy ending. I wasn't sure I could make it happen, but I wanted to try.

I realized that my plan to offer a donation was naïve. Also, I could have easily ended up pissing him off when he found out that the million dollars was bait to get to know him.

There was always the straightforward approach. Tell him the truth.

Sometimes we try too hard. The truth looked so simple and just thinking about it lifted the weight from my heart. No need to concoct a master lie of colorful lies.

So I wrote him an email. I told him who I was and why I was looking for him. I told him that I would be getting a huge amount of money that I already planned to give away to charity. I told him I was afraid he wouldn't respond so I used the donation as bait. It took me a long time to decide to use this word. I added that I'm sorry if it sucked, but I really wanted to get to know him and I really wanted to make a donation.

I sent the email and felt great. I assumed it would take him days to answer, but to my huge surprise he answered right back.

Hi Alexa,

I'm still in town. Actually, I'm in an internet café working on my blog, so I thought I'd answer you right away. First off, thank you for your candid email and your interest in me. I understand your curiosity. I guess that we are technically related because my biological mother is in fact your Aunt Darlene. As you might know, I was given up for adoption at the tender age of three weeks, and since my first memory, I was loved and raised by great parents. Being born to your aunt is a fact that never had any meaning to me and never will. I have to admit that her appearance in my life became pretty annoying and I made it clear to her that I did not wish to have any relationship with her whatsoever. When she found me, I was in a phase of my life that wasn't great, to say the least. I managed to pull myself out of it and start a new, meaningful life. It's a long story. I guess that looking for me also brought new meaning to Darlene's life. But this is her business and her life. Or her art. Or all of the above.

I'm teaching in a school that my organization has built here after the earthquake, in a village on the north side of the island. People here are poor. Very poor. They were in bad shape before the earthquake, and ironically in the last ten years they have gotten an opportunity to better themselves because the world started to show interest. The reality is harsh here, but each passing day we see another ray of hope, we experience another opening, and take another step forward. Each day I do something that makes my pupils' lives brighter. And I'm thankful for that. This is my reality.

One day you should come and see what we do here. Regardless of our 'biological relation,' I'd be happy to stay in touch with you. You seem like a cool kid.

Best, Joe.

I read it again. And again. And again. I was sooo happy.
I wrote back,

Dear Joe,

In my opinion we are officially friends. I'll write you from time to time (I'm not going to bother you, I promise.). If you happen to be in LA let me know.

And you might be surprised—I might come over to your school one day and pay you a visit.

Yours,

Alexa

P.S. I'll take care of the donation with Ms. Roberts.

A STAR IS REBORN

People who hate LA complain that the weather here is boring. They whine that all we have here is an eternal spring. What about the seasonal changes, they ask. What about the autumn? It's so beautiful back east. The colors of the sky, the leaves falling in slow motion, until this ideal weather is interrupted by a live broadcast about the worst storm in history that is about to hit them hard. They give their storms funny names of old ladies but what you see on TV is far from being funny. It is pretty miserable.

In my opinion, there is the world (yawn), and then the United States (boring), and then California (who cares?), and then LA (pretty okay), and then Beverly Hills (awesome).

It's the magic hour now. The sky is purple, the sun is setting, the light is soft and the world seems at peace. Poetic, isn't it? Inside the Goldsmith mansion, Mom screams at her makeup artist. "You ruined it! You dumb cow!" and I know that life is great, everything is normal, and we are the luckiest family on earth.

I'm in my room waiting for a knock on the door; a young PA fresh out of film school is about to invite me to shoot my Catwoman part.

But he is late.

I had been reading about Haiti for a while, and a couple of hours later, I realized that I had been forgotten.

I looked out the window. Something strange was happening.

The entire *Cruella* crew had disappeared as if abducted by a huge flying saucer that was so quiet I didn't even notice.

"What's going on?" I texted Mom, but there was no answer.

I went downstairs and found some production assistants packing in the kitchen.

"Where is everyone?" I asked.

"We are moving to another location," one of them said.

"But I was supposed to be next up," I said. "What about my shoot?"

He shrugged. "Something urgent came up. I don't know what. They just said that we are shooting at Gale Studios in Hollywood and everyone has to move there. I'm going there in ten."

"Can you take me there?" I asked.

"Sure," he said.

We drove in his beat-up car through heavy rush hour traffic and it took us forty-five minutes to get to the studios.

I saw Mike pacing in the parking lot and ran up to him. "Hey, Mike, where is everyone?"

He was surprised to see me. Even behind his Ray-Bans and poker-face.

"What are you doing here?" he said. "You are not supposed to be here."

"What's going on?" I begged. "Tell me!"

He shrugged. "They're shooting a scene for the finale." "Why didn't anyone tell me? Why the rush?"

He took a big breath as if he had made his decision. "Why don't you go inside and see for yourself?"

He walked me into the building and pointed to one of the soundstage doors. "Keep me out of it please," he said.

I pushed the big doors, disregarding the red light, passed a few crew members and entered a set that was a replica of a hospital room. My heart raced. The lights were bright and when I came closer it was clear that I had burst onto the set in the middle of a take.

I couldn't believe my eyes. Mom was sitting by the bed. She was talking to someone who was lying there.

I freaked out. The set was exactly like Ian's hospital room. The monitors, the IV, the TV set, even the beige curtains.

No one saw me; everyone's eyes were on the bed.

I took a few paces towards Bruce's monitor and stood behind him.

Glancing at the monitor made me want to scream.

Mom was talking to someone who looked like Ian's clone.

She said in her most soothing voice, "Ian, please wake up. I pray every day for your recovery. You are too young to die. Ian, I'm begging you." Her voice got harder, infused with urgency. "Ian, I'm commanding you. Open your eyes."

The camera zoomed into the person's face. His eyes were closed.

I thought I was dreaming. How the hell had they found someone who looked exactly like Ian?

"Please, Ian," Mom repeated. "You have to open your eyes and come back to us. I order you to do it."

It was insane. One eyelash moved. And then another. I couldn't breathe.

The person in the bed opened his eyes.

"Yes!" Mom raised her voice. "Yes," she said. "You are back! You are back!" she said as she held his hand.

"Where am I?" the person whispered gravely.

"You came back to life, Ian," Mom said. "You were on the other side for a very long time."

The person looked as if he wanted to say something.

"Damn," he said finally, "I forgot my lines."

"Still rolling!" Bruce called.

"Keep quiet. We are still rolling!" the first AD announced.

I heard Mom saying, "No worries, Ian. You are doing well for someone who was in a coma for sixty long days. Let's just do it one more time."

"Yeah, I'm tired," Ian whispered. "I need some rest." He closed his eyes and dozed off.

"Doctor!" Mom yelled.

A man in a suit, whom I assume was a physician, rushed over to the bed and started to give him a check-up.

It seemed crazy. Beyond belief. But in our family, *everything* was crazy and beyond belief.

I ran over to the bed and touched my brother's hand.

"Ian, it's me, Alexa!"

He opened one eye. "Sister," he whispered with a shred of a smile. "Where have you been?"

And closed his eyes again.

I cried out. "Ian, come back!"

"He's going to be okay," the doctor said. "Just give him time. He needs some rest."

I saw Mom's face above me. Her face was red and not just because of the heavy-duty make up she wore. She was angry because of my unannounced visit.

But she was all business. "Cut!" she yelled at Bruce. "I need a minute here!"

"I don't have time to waste," Mom told the physician. "We have a show to finish. Make it happen!"

"I'm trying," he said in an obedient tone.

She turned to me. "Why are you here?" she demanded. "You are not supposed to be here!"

"What's going on?" I screamed, "Ian should be in the hospital!"

"He is back to normal, almost," Mom said. "He is out of his coma. Aren't you happy?"

"Why is he here?" I yelled. "He isn't well!"

"Keep your voice down," she said briskly. "He always wanted to star in the show. So I'm making him a star in the finale. America is going to see your brother coming back from the dead. He'll be alive and well and very famous. This is what he always wanted!"

Ian opened his eyes and winked. "I'm going to be a star," he whispered. "This is the best moment of my life."

"See?" Mom said victoriously.

I was overjoyed and I was angry, I was humiliated and I was elated. It was too confusing and it was way too much for me to handle.

I stormed off the set and called Dad. I told him what just happened and he freaked out.

"I'm coming right now," he yelled. "That woman is nuts!"

"I know," I said, "But Dad?"

"Yes?" he said, short of breath. "Cheer up!" I said, "Ian is back!"

AN ALMOST HAPPY ENDING

About a month later, Dad submitted the first draft of *The Smart Rebellion* and filed for divorce on the same day.

Summer was approaching fast and I was getting ready to go on a trip.

One day after school I asked Carlos to take me to Venice Beach. On my way we stopped at Starbucks and I bought an extra strong cappuccino to go.

I met Roberta on the beach. We sat on a bench under a palm tree. She looked horrible, as if she hadn't slept for a week, and she smelled bad. Her cart was full of junk. I handed her the coffee and she thanked me with a wide smile.

A couple of weeks earlier I wrote her that I'd like to see her. Last night she called and asked me to come down.

I told her about Joe, her son. How I tracked him down, and when I talked she gave me her full attention until I was done talking. Her face didn't show any emotion, as if she was unmoved by my story. Or maybe she was hiding her feelings. I didn't know for sure.

"I'm very proud of you," she said in her calm voice, "You have changed a lot. You grew up since the last time I saw you. It's your journey and I admire you, Alexa, because you made it so meaningful. You made up your mind to donate a million dollars to charity and go to Haiti in the summer. Wow. It's great. You are great. Really."

She sipped from the cup of cappuccino.

"Thank you," I said. "But what do you think about what I told you, about Joe?"

She looked at me with a glint in her eyes. "One day, a few years ago, I separated from a man I was in love with for many years. It was a painful experience and it brought me back to the one thing I had been trying to avoid my whole life. The question that was haunting me every day since I gave up my baby for adoption. What happened to Max? That is what

I named him. Max. I felt that the time was right, that in order to save myself I needed to find him. So I started to search and found out that he was here in LA, homeless and broken, desperate and depressed. He was at the lowest point in his life, and I was at the lowest point in my life. I felt that this would be where the two of us could reconnect. Apparently it was dumb and selfish of me. I wanted to reach out to him, so instead of bursting into his life, I decided to live like him. Go down and live a homeless life, get to know him and make friends before letting him know who I was. It looked romantic but foolish nonetheless. And I did it for a while and it was horrible and startling and life-changing. I got to know him by roaming in his territory. And then one day I made my move. It was a stormy day, and we stayed together in the shelter. I started to talk to him, trying in a terrible awkward way to tell him who I was. He didn't want to listen. He yelled at me. He told me that he had two great parents. He was angry. I tried to explain why I had come down, why I lived like a homeless person, but it only made him angrier. He told me I was a fraud, rude and crazy, and he didn't want anything to do with me. I felt horrible. I wanted to restart the conversation. I wanted to explain that I was just asking for a chance to get to know him but he told me to go to hell and the next day he disappeared. Vanished into thin air. I stayed there for three months, walking the streets he used to walk, befriending his buddies, hoping he'd show up, because I wanted to have another shot at talking to him. But he was gone for good. Even your grandpa couldn't find him. Then one day I just gave up and went home. That was when I started to paint. I had painted before, as a hobby, but this time it became the main thing in my life. Immersing myself in my art saved me. Later, I felt the urge to go down again. Go back to the gutter, to the pavement, to the people I left behind. It wasn't about Max anymore, or Joe, it was about me. And then I realized that it was always about me. He was right to reject me. I was selfish. And he was right."

"But maybe someday he'll change his mind," I said in a trembling voice.

She looked at me and I saw in her eyes that she had given up. "I'm glad he found his calling," she said, "Good for him. Joe is a stranger to me, just as I am a stranger to Joe. But no one can take Max from me. Ever."

I didn't know what to say.

"I told you before," she said with a smile, "Most of us are broken and all our lives we try to find the broken pieces and glue them back together. We do it in order to understand who we are, and why we are here, and to figure out if there is a purpose. So I suppose this is my way of doing it. Trying to answer those questions with my art, and by being here."

I thought about it for a minute. "I went after Joe because I thought you wanted me to dig into your past and find him. And when I found him I was so excited to reunite the two of you. And now the whole thing feels so useless." I was disappointed and she realized that.

"Looking for Joe was my story, and you started your own. This is what people do. We need to create stories for ourselves because otherwise life would be so very boring." She chuckled as if it was funny, but I knew she didn't think it was funny.

I recorded the entire conversation. I knew that I would listen to it many times because I didn't totally grasp everything she said.

"So how are you?" I asked because I didn't have a better question.

"I feel right," she said. There was no happiness in her voice and no sadness. And I wondered if feeling right meant not feeling at all.

"Take off your shoes," she said.

I did and we both went to the water. I felt the hot sand tingling my feet. And then came the cold water of the ocean. It felt good.

"What a beautiful day," she said. I nodded.

Cruella's finale broke the all-time ratings record. The scene where Mom made her stepson wake up from his coma became a YouTube sensation. In reality—the real reality—he woke up from his coma the night before, and Mom got word from the nurses she had hired to get Dad away from the hospital and to inform her when Ian woke up. She hurried to the hospital in the middle of the night and convinced Ian to do the show. A day later, she moved him out of the hospital and into the studio, telling the hospital that she was moving him to another hospital. It was deranged and dangerous, but she only cared about her show and poor Ian was just along for the ride. After she got everything she needed on tape, Ian was taken to the new hospital and a week later he came back home. Not to his Silver Lake apartment, but to our house, where he could be taken care of, or as Mom told everyone, "Be a part of the creative process of *Cruella's* second season."

This was great news to me. I was absent from the finale and no one cared. No one mentioned my name when they discussed the next season, which was great because all I wanted was to be left alone. I was glad that my brother lived with us. He took over Dad's shack and his recovery was speedy indeed.

When I turned twelve on June fourth, we had a small birthday celebration. For a brief two hours we looked like a normal family again. And I was happy to have with me two honorary guests, Justin and Guy.

When my two buddies showed up, Justin asked me to show him around the house. Guy bailed because "he did the tour already," and stayed in my room.

Birthday dinner was an hour away. "I didn't think you were into this stuff," I protested when we were walking through the house.

"Into what?" he gave me a puzzled look.

"Rich people's houses and a showy car collection," I said. "I'm not," he said. "But still…"

I wanted to skip Mom's bedroom but the door was half open and he just went in. I rushed after him and pulled his arm toward the door.

"I'm impressed," he said. He was staring at her shrine, the wall with all her clippings and pictures.

"Don't be," I said.

"I bet your mom is cooler than you would ever admit," he said.

"Why?"

"Because we tend to underestimate our parents."

I dragged him out of her bedroom. "Speak for yourself," I said.

When we were in the corridor he said, "I heard that there was a terrible accident at one of your birthday parties when you were little."

"Oh," I said. "I don't like to talk about it, especially not on my birthday."

"A birthday guest disappeared in the house," he said with a grave tone.

"Yeah," I said.

"Never to be found," he continued.

"Right," I said.

"It's a sad story," he said and winked.

"Yes, it is," I agreed. Although I had made up the story, I felt a shiver down my spine whenever I pictured the kid's skeleton waiting to be found in one of the closets. I know it's weird.

But still.

"Don't tell anyone, but I made it up," I said.

"Why'd you do that?" he asked with a smile.

"Once, when I was five or six, I heard that a kid drowned in a pool at a birthday party. It haunted me. I couldn't fall asleep for many nights. Ever since, I tried to avoid birthday parties, pool parties, any party. I'm a party pooper. I know. Maybe making up the story was a way of laughing it off."

He looked surprised. "What about tonight?"

"I hope you and Guy find your way out, now that I showed you the house," I said trying to lighten the conversation.

I looked at his eyes trying to tell him something but he wasn't looking at me. He was texting feverishly.

I walked down the stairs. Dinner was almost ready.

After dinner Mom asked everyone to come outside by the pool. Gabby and Rosie brought the cake, and I blew out the candles and closed my eyes and made a wish. Behind the trees, on the hill above the house, a fireworks show began. The fireworks were amazing. A rainbow of colors lit the sky, and when I saw Mom smiling at me proudly I knew it was her idea.

I smiled back, and then I looked around, just to make sure that there were no hidden cameras.

No one asked me how I felt. Maybe because they were afraid to know the truth. Or maybe because they assumed I felt great.

The truth was, I felt right. I made a few good choices and I didn't need a mask anymore.

I was okay without the web of colorful lies, and what was even more gratifying, I felt that I had found my true colors. As Roberta said, I was writing my own story.

The last fireworks explosion was spectacular. All of us clapped enthusiastically and then the illuminated sky darkened and Mumford and Sons started to play over the loudspeakers.

I looked at Justin. He smiled and began walking towards me. I felt happy and a bit choked up. I was feeling something I had never felt before and it made me shiver. I tried to resist it but he was already standing next to me.

"You are a-a-amazing," he said.

I didn't think, the words just floated and there was no way back.

"I love you, too," I said.

www.ingramcontent.com/pod-product-compliance
Lightning Source LLC
Chambersburg PA
CBHW050820180626
46814CB00004B/1375